"El Gato cond[...] school for his sub p[...]"

Mack Bolan pondered Ramirez's words. It made perfect sense. The drug lord could hardly advertise for sub drivers in the classifieds. Quesada would employ one or two experts who would train those who heard of the positions through criminal contacts.

The Executioner swung the binoculars around the perimeter of the lake, noting a cliff pockmarked with caves, the biggest of them at water level. Within it was a hint of movement.

"Señor!" Lazalde said urgently.

Bolan gazed across the water. He didn't need the binoculars to see that the four minisubs had changed direction, that their new heading was taking them straight toward the patrol boat.

MACK BOLAN ®

The Executioner

DON PENDLETON'S
THE EXECUTIONER®
DEEP ATTACK

A GOLD EAGLE BOOK FROM
WORLDWIDE®

TORONTO • NEW YORK • LONDON
AMSTERDAM • PARIS • SYDNEY • HAMBURG
STOCKHOLM • ATHENS • TOKYO • MILAN
MADRID • WARSAW • BUDAPEST • AUCKLAND

First edition February 1998
ISBN 0-373-64230-X

Special thanks and acknowledgment to
David Robbins for his contribution to this work.

DEEP ATTACK

When bad men combine, the good must associate, else they will fall one by one, an unpitied sacrifice in a contemptible struggle.

—Edmund Burke
"Thoughts on the Cause of Present Discontent,"
April 23, 1770

When those who govern come under suspicion of betraying the people they are sworn to represent, they'd better stand up under scrutiny or suffer the consequences of their actions.

—Mack Bolan

THE

LEGEND

Nothing less than a war could have fashioned the destiny of the man called Mack Bolan. Bolan earned the Executioner title in the jungle hell of Vietnam.

But this soldier also wore another name—Sergeant Mercy. He was so tagged because of the compassion he showed to wounded comrades-in-arms and Vietnamese civilians.

Mack Bolan's second tour of duty ended prematurely when he was given emergency leave to return home and bury his family, victims of the Mob. Then he declared a one-man war against the Mafia.

He confronted the Families head-on from coast to coast, and soon a hope of victory began to appear. But Bolan had broken society's every rule. That same society started gunning for this elusive warrior—to no avail.

So Bolan was offered amnesty to work within the system against terrorism. This time, as an employee of Uncle Sam, Bolan became Colonel John Phoenix. With a command center at Stony Man Farm in Virginia, he and his new allies—Able Team and Phoenix Force—waged relentless war on a new adversary: the KGB.

But when his one true love, April Rose, died at the hands of the Soviet terror machine, Bolan severed all ties with Establishment authority.

Now, after a lengthy lone-wolf struggle and much soul-searching, the Executioner has agreed to enter an "arm's-length" alliance with his government once more, reserving the right to pursue personal missions in his Everlasting War.

PROLOGUE

It was a routine patrol out of Alameda Coast Guard Base. No one was supposed to die.

Coast Guard patrol boat CG 30390 cruised northward at twenty knots. Lieutenant George Bergan was in no great hurry. He had all night to put the new boat through its paces and make note of any bugs for the ratings to repair after he returned to base.

Bergan stared at the inky stretch of sea to the north. On moonless, overcast nights like this one, the Pacific Ocean was like an endless expanse of black satin.

He cocked an eye at the younger man fidgeting beside him. "Relax, Pullman," he said, smirking. "I very much doubt we'll have to respond to any major disasters during our shift."

Ensign Ernest Pullman was fresh out of the academy. He had recently been assigned to Alameda, and this was his first time on patrol. Absently nodding, he said, "But what about drug smugglers, sir? I hear that patrols run into them all the time out here."

"You've been listening to too much galley scuttlebutt. Yes, we do run into smugglers on occasion, but it's not as if we have raging gun battles every night. Smugglers aren't fools, Ensign. They know that our boats are as fast as anything they can put in the water, and they know our surveillance and detection equipment is state-of-the-art."

As if to emphasize that fact, the sonar operator piped up, "Lieutenant, we've picked up a target off the starboard bow."

Bergan scanned the murky shoreline but saw no evidence of running lights. "Range and bearing, Seaman?"

"Range is one-zero-nine-zero. It's not moving at the moment, sir. But—"

The sonarman's indecision was unusual. Seaman Timmons had always impressed Bergan as being extremely competent. "But what?" he prompted.

"Well, sir, it must be a glitch, yet I'd swear that when I first picked it up, the prop emissions were subsurface. Now they're *on* the surface."

Bergan had a decision to make. Should they continue with their routine run or investigate? He was inclined to think it was a fisherman or else a yachtsman out of San Francisco. But the eager look on Pullman's face persuaded him to make sure. If nothing else, the disappointment might calm the ensign down.

"Hard to starboard, ahead flank speed," Bergan ordered. "All hands to duty stations. Kill all lights until we're right on them."

A bustle of activity broke out. The bridge darkened except for the pale green-and-red glow of instrument panels.

Timmons reported again. "Range is one thousand

yards, sir. The target is still holding steady. It's in a deep cove, depth about three hundred.''

"Configuration?" Bergan requested.

"Narrow beam, sir. Eighty feet, overall. Twin screws to stern."

The helmsman broke in. "Sir, look!" He pointed over the bow.

The officer's pulse quickened. A pinpoint of light flashed from side to side three times on a knobby spine of land and was answered by the target craft.

"A signal!" Pullman stated the obvious.

Timmons had more to add. "Target is moving, now, sir. Less than a knot, making for shore."

A tingle ran down Bergan's spine. The mystery boat behaved quite suspiciously. Maybe there was more to this than he had thought. "Mr. Pullman, you will lead the boarding party yourself. First make sure every man on board has his side arm and that the boarding party have their M-16s locked and loaded."

"Aye, sir!" the ensign eagerly replied, and took off like a greyhound, bumping the bulwark in his haste to get out the door.

Shaking his head in amusement, Bergan took a night-vision scope from the console and trained it on the dark shoreline. The patrol boat was still too far out for him to note much detail. It occurred to him that he should contact Alameda and let the base know what was happening. But if it turned out to be a false alarm, there would be hell to pay with the captain. Better, he reasoned, to check out the situation first, then report in.

"Read off the range, Mr. Timmons," the officer directed.

"About nine hundred yards, and closing fast." There was a pause. "Eight hundred." Another pause. "Seven hundred."

At a range of five hundred yards, Bergan peered through the scope again. The passive system didn't rely on infrared or other enhancements. It simply amplified the ambient light to the point where it seemed as if he were viewing the scene in broad daylight.

The moment Bergan spotted the target, he gave the order to reduce speed to five knots. His plan was to sneak in and catch the culprits, if such they were, napping. Two seamen manned spotlights, awaiting his command to switch them on.

"The target has stopped again, sir," the sonarman reported.

Bergan leaned forward as the patrol boat cleared the cove entrance. Finally he saw the target clearly. It had a narrow beam, all right, and was low in the water. Much too low to be any conventional craft that he knew of.

"What is it?" Bergan said aloud. He mentally reviewed the duty log, trying to recall if there had been any mention of the Navy conducting maneuvers in the area.

The Coast Guard vessel closed to within 150 yards.

"Sir!" Timmon's voice rang out crisply. "Screw emissions have doubled. It's coming about."

Sure enough, Bergan saw the target knife the water

smoothly in a tight arc. At the same time, it began to dip below the surface.

Excitement tinged the sonar operator's tone. "Target is diving!"

Bergan could scarcely credit his eyes. Already the other craft was nearly under water. The periscope and antenna array jutted skyward like the spines of an aquatic lizard. "This can't be!" he breathed in astonishment.

"Target is at twenty feet and still going down!" Timmons disclosed. "Bearing has changed."

"Heading?" Bergan asked, certain the craft would try to slip around them to gain the open sea.

"It's coming right at us, sir! Speed is ten knots and climbing rapidly."

"Spotlights!" Bergan barked. Immediately twin brilliant beams flashed out over the area in front of their vessel. There was no trace of the target other than a faint ripple where it had gone under. "Timmons! Is it breaking to the right or the left?"

"Neither, sir! It's still heading straight at us!"

"Helmsman, hard to port!"

The vessel sloughed sharply to the left, but it was too little, too late. The words were barely out of Bergan's mouth when the sonar operator bawled, "Sir! Target has fired a—"

A tremendous explosion shredded the patrol boat as if it were so much kindling, lifting it clear out of the water and engulfing it in a roiling fireball. Bit by bit, small and large pieces of debris rained to the ocean surface.

Among them were charred limbs and shattered torsos.

1

The hunter was being hunted.

Mack Bolan couldn't say exactly when he picked up the tail. The first inkling he had was when he idly glanced into a storefront window and noticed a gangly scarecrow half a block back, watching him intently.

It had to be an amateur. No pro would get that close or be so obvious.

Bolan strolled down the side street as if he hadn't noticed. Hands thrust in his pockets, he rounded the next corner and promptly picked up the pace, weaving among the pedestrians.

It was late afternoon in Key West. Tourists roamed the street in droves, soaking up the Florida sunshine. Under different circumstances, Bolan might have been inclined to admire the many attractive women who strolled around in skimpy bathing suits. But as it was, he had something more important on his mind. Namely staying alive.

Ducking into the recessed doorway of a clothing store, the Executioner pressed back into the shadows. He didn't have long to wait. The tail rushed past, glancing right and left, never giving the doorway a second look. Bolan stayed put for about ten seconds, then warily climbed the short flight of steps.

The tail had reached the next corner and was turning every which way, clearly upset. He wore jeans and a brown short-sleeved shirt that revealed a tattoo on his left arm. A faded cap perched atop a tangle of sandy hair.

When the man moved on, Bolan followed. He was very interested in learning who the guy worked for and how they had found out about him.

His visit to southern Florida was known only to a select few. His good friends Hal Brognola, director of the Justice Department's Sensitive Operations Group, and Barbara Price, mission controller at Stony Man Farm, were aware of Bolan's whereabouts. Clearly, so was someone else.

A new drug pipeline was in operation. According to the DEA, cocaine in record quantities was being funneled through the Keys onto the mainland. Key West was believed to be the relay point, but the authorities had no idea how the coke was being brought in.

At Brognola's request, Bolan was there to find out how and to put the pipeline out of business. Acting on a lead supplied by the big Fed, he was close to nailing the people responsible. But now it appeared that they were also on to him.

True to form, the tail never thought to look back. He scoured every side street he passed, growing more and more agitated. At a seafood restaurant, he ducked inside.

Bolan crossed the street. From behind a parked

van, he peered into the restaurant and saw his quarry on a pay phone by the large front window.

Judging by the man's expression and gestures, he was extremely upset. At length the tail jammed down the phone and stalked from the building.

The soldier let the man gain a good lead before trailing. Staying a block back at all times, Bolan made it a point to always keep a pedestrian or two between them. They soon neared the docks. When the tail turned onto a walk leading to a shabby two-story building, the Executioner sank onto one knee and pretended to tie a shoe.

The man never bothered to knock. He walked in as if he owned the place, slamming the door behind him.

Rising, Bolan retraced his steps to the last junction, crossed and kept going for a whole block. A turn to the right took him to the rear of the building, which was even shabbier than the front. Paint had peeled from the walls, and one of the bottom windows was cracked.

Bolan slipped a hand under his jacket and loosened his 9 mm Beretta in its speed rig under his left arm.

He looked both ways to verify no one was watching, then gripped the top of the waist-high picket fence and vaulted over. Crouching in a cluster of bushes, he listened for an alarm.

Evidently no one had noticed him. Bolan crept to the back door. He gingerly turned the knob, discovering it was unlocked. But before barging in, he moved to the left and stopped next to the cracked window.

A shade had been drawn. Somewhere inside, two people were arguing. Their voices were muffled but loud enough for Bolan to catch every word.

"—off my case, will you? I'm telling you that the guy couldn't have known I was dogging him. It was a fluke he disappeared, is all."

"A fluke?" the second man repeated. "What do you use for brains, Sammy? The chump made you and took a powder. And now Santoro is going to be ticked off when he finds out you blew it."

"I'm not scared of Santoro."

"You should be. He's mean, friend. He'd as soon gut you as look at you. Word is, he killed his own brother when he thought the guy was skimming." The second man snickered. "Turned out the brother hadn't been cheating at all. It was someone else. When Santoro found out, he took the fella out into the Everglades and fed him to the gators, one piece at a time."

"Talk, Baker. That's all it is," Sammy said, but he didn't sound convincing.

The voices dwindled. Bolan returned to the back door and was about to enter when he heard footsteps approaching the other side.

"What I'm saying, man, is that you'd better hope Santoro is in a good mood. He pays us good money to take care of problems like this, and he won't like you blowing it."

Bolan whirled. He had to find a place to hide, and quickly, but the weed-choked lawn offered little concealment. He raced around the corner of the building just as the door opened.

Baker was a swarthy, thickset man with hands the size of hams. He wore a light jacket despite the temperature, a telltale bulge under his right arm providing the reason. Carrying a bulging green garbage bag, he went to a trash can at the curb and deposited it.

Sammy the tail waited in the doorway. "If you ask me, we should pack up and head for the mainland. Pickings are slim here in the Keys. You know that. We were lucky to connect with Santoro's people or we'd be out mugging tourists for spending money."

"Gripe, gripe, gripe," Baker said.

"Do you have a better idea?"

"As a matter of fact, I do. We'll stay on another six months or so, do a few more jobs for Santoro and squirrel away enough dough to tide us over for a while in Miami."

"Six more months?" Sammy said. "I don't know. That's a long time."

Bolan wasted no more time eavesdropping in the hope they might reveal pertinent intel. Baker was returning. Sprinting to the front of the house, he cracked the front door. Sammy stood at the far end of a narrow hall, his back to the Executioner.

Slipping inside, Bolan ducked into the first room he came to, which turned out to be a living room, as cheaply furnished as any cut-rate motel.

An open closet grabbed his attention, and he hurried inside. No sooner had Bolan pulled the door almost closed than the sound of someone with a heavy tread confirmed the hardmen were back. He could have taken them out then and there, but he needed more information to go on other than the name Santoro.

It was a name Bolan had heard before. The word on the street was that José Santoro had the local coke market cornered and was the main player in smuggling huge quantities of the drug stateside. But no one seemed to know where Santoro lived, or his favorite night spots. Fear had a lot to do with the widespread amnesia. Like Baker, everyone was deathly afraid of the man.

But Bolan had found a boat-charter operator who wasn't.

Just then, pots rattled, a cupboard door squeaked and a chair scraped across a floor. The two men were making supper.

Bolan aligned an ear to the crack. He could hear the pair talking but not loudly enough to make out what they were saying. After a minute went by, he quietly padded to the hallway. Light spilling from a room twenty feet away revealed the location of the kitchen.

The soldier catfooted to the door. Sammy was complaining about a hike in the price of his favorite beer, then in the next breath said, "What time do we meet with Santoro?"

"At nine."

"His place, or the boat?"

Bolan's interest peaked. If he shadowed them when they left, the men would lead him right to the man he was after. He waited for the reply, which never came. The phone in the living room rang, and before Bolan could vacate the hall, Sammy rushed out of the kitchen, and they almost collided.

Rooted in place for a moment, Sammy reached under his baggy shirt and produced a .40-caliber SIG-Sauer P-229 pistol.

The soldier reacted automatically. Grabbing the gunner's wrist, he wrenched it even as he slid in close and drove a knee into the thin man's groin. Sammy sputtered, his face scarlet, and went momentarily limp.

Bolan slammed his adversary against the wall, then delivered a palm-heel strike to the nose. Cartilage shattered and blood spurted over the gunner's chest. Sammy sagged, his eyelids fluttering. One more blow would render him unconscious. But as the Executioner drew back his hand, a 275-pound human bull barreled out of the kitchen and plowed into him.

Bolan was hurled into the opposite wall so hard that the breath was knocked out of him. Agony seared his backbone. Arms as thick as pythons looped around his waist and hoisted him off the floor as effortlessly as he might lift a child.

"Bad move coming here, chump!" Baker growled. "I recognize you from Mr. Santoro's description." Hissing, he tightened his grip. "Santoro wants to learn why you've been asking so many questions around Key West. Care to tell me?"

Bolan recovered enough to land a solid right to the bruiser's jaw. It was like punching a brick wall. Baker laughed off the blow, gritted his teeth and strained. The soldier arched his back as pain speared through him.

"Hurting yet, sucker?" Baker taunted. "By the time I'm done, every rib will be busted and your insides will be mush. Spare yourself some grief and tell me what Santoro wants to hear."

The hardman talked too much. Bolan had used the precious seconds to brace his feet against the wall. Suddenly pushing off with all his might, he propelled Baker backward. The gunner tried to set himself, but the next moment he tripped over his partner, who had slumped to his knees and was wheezing hoarsely.

Baker toppled, throwing his hands behind him to cushion his fall.

Taking instant advantage, Bolan dropped into a crouch. Baker shoved up off the floor, but he wasn't fast enough. The Executioner landed two swift punches that flattened the powerhouse. Yet Baker was far from out. His legs, as sturdy as tree trunks, lashed out, catching Bolan full on the sternum.

As if fired from a catapult, Bolan was flung over six feet and hit the floor on his shoulders. As fluidly as an acrobat, he rolled onto the balls of his feet to surge erect.

Baker stormed forward, unleashing a flurry of blows that would have rendered most adversaries senseless.

Not the Executioner, though. He had honed his skills on the killing fields of the world, learning moves that would have been the envy of any seasoned street fighter. He slipped the first punch, blocked a second and retaliated by hopping into the air and pounding his knee into Baker's jaw. The husky hardman staggered but still didn't go down.

Bolan drove a snap kick into Baker's gut that had no effect. The man's stomach was as hard as nails. Baker rumbled deep in his barrel chest, like an enraged bear, then threw himself at his opponent with his arms spread wide.

The soldier skipped backward to keep out of reach and came to a doorway. Gripping the jamb, he swung into the room. But then, instead of letting go, he swiveled and reversed direction, his legs locked and rigid.

Baker rushed in. He was struck in the ribs and went flying, smashing into the hall wall. It seemed as if the entire house shook. Tossing his head, he growled and renewed his attack, cautiously this time, his ham-sized fists poised.

Bolan moved to the center of the room where he had space to maneuver. On his right was a bed, on his left a dresser littered with a pen, pencils and paper. Slightly behind him and to the right was a wooden chair.

Dark eyes agleam with feral blood lust, Baker charged. Suddenly pivoting, Bolan grabbed the chair and swept it up, putting everything he had into his swing. The chair's legs shattered against Baker's upturned face, and he roared in pain and rage.

Blood seeping from a split eyebrow, Baker bared his teeth and snarled, "Santoro can forget about questioning you. You're all mine, and I'm going to grind you to a pulp!"

So far Bolan had only been trying to knock out the husky bruiser. He had questions of his own that needed answering. But it began to look as if the only way he would stop Baker was to kill him. Determined to give it one last try, Bolan cast about for something else he could use to bring the hulk down.

The instant the soldier's gaze shifted from Baker, the man struck. For such a massive person, he could move incredibly quickly. He was on Bolan in a twinkling. The Executioner tried a spear-hand thrust to the throat, but Baker twisted so that Bolan's fingers merely brushed his neck.

"None of your fancy moves will work with me, Fed!"

Bolan countered a series of brutal punches. In doing so, he was forced to retreat, and a second later found himself boxed in a corner.

Pausing, Baker grinned sadistically. "You have nowhere left to run, and you sure as hell aren't getting past me."

The comment gave the soldier an idea. Since the bruiser liked to talk so much, maybe Bolan could use that to his advantage. "How about we make a deal?" he asked.

Baker blinked. "A deal? Your back is to the wall and you want to cut *me* some slack?" He thought the notion so funny that he threw back his head and laughed.

Which was exactly the opening that Bolan needed. Taking a swift step, he rammed his right heel on the tip of Baker's toes.

There was a loud crack, and Baker's mirth choked

off. Flushing crimson, he roared in pain. "You broke my damn foot!"

That wasn't all Bolan intended to do. Dropping low, he placed his palms flat on the floor and levered his legs around in a blur. His shins caught Baker behind the knees, sweeping the man off his feet.

Bolan's right hand darted under his jacket as Baker sat up. Three times in swift succession he smashed the barrel across the guy's forehead. On the third blow, Baker uttered a grunt, closed his eyes and sank onto the floor.

The soldier heard a metallic click coming from the hall. Without hesitation he dived over Baker's prone form, and as he landed on his stomach, he pointed the Beretta at the man framed in the doorway.

Sammy held the SIG-Sauer in a two-handed grip. His face plastered with blood, his mouth twitching in rage, he stroked the trigger twice.

Slugs chewed into the floorboards in front of Bolan's face. Ignoring them, he answered in kind, the parabellum rounds jackknifing the skinny hardman into the wall.

Sammy slid downward, leaving a scarlet smear in his wake. Somehow he was able to lift his pistol. His arm shook terribly, but he was determined to get off one more shot.

Bolan wasn't about to let him. He fired a single round and a neat hole blossomed between the gunner's eyes.

Sammy's head cracked back against the wall. His body convulsed for a few moments, then was still.

Slowly rising, Bolan moved to the body and verified there was no pulse. He quickly went through the corpse's pockets. A wallet contained seventy dollars in small bills, a driver's license and a photograph of a smiling woman, but not a single clue as to where Bolan could locate José Santoro.

The soldier sighed and stood. It hadn't been a total loss. He still had Baker. In time, the man would talk. He started to turn but wasn't quite all the way around when an express train hurtled into him. Baker's bulk mashed him into the wall, jarring the Beretta from his grasp. Pinwheels of light exploded before his eyes, and the hallway seemed to spin like a tornado.

"You *die,* scumbag!" Baker rasped in his ear.

Iron fingers clamped on Bolan's neck from behind. They gouged into him and began to twist. With a start, Bolan realized the bruiser was trying to snap his spine. He jabbed an elbow into Baker's side, but to no avail.

Bolan tried to stand, but Baker held him down. He tried to turn, but the man wouldn't allow him. Pushing against the wall did no good, either. Baker was as immovable as a mountain. And all the while, those iron fingers gouged deeper and deeper.

Acute pain racked Bolan, and a red haze shrouded his mind. Unless he did something soon, he'd be unconscious. He groped along the floor, seeking the Beretta. His fingers closed on a gun, but it wasn't his. Not that it mattered.

Bolan managed to shift enough to see Baker's smirking face. Whipping up his arm, he fired at point-blank range. His adversary's right eyeball burst. For a few moments, though, nothing happened.

Only when the soldier tore loose and rose did the thickset body keel over, landing on top of Sammy's.

He frowned. All that effort, and he was left empty-handed. He hoped it wasn't an omen.

2

A blazing red sun rested on the western rim of the world when Mack Bolan arrived at the pier. Out on the tranquil gulf, fishing craft bearing sunburned tourists were returning from a long day at sea. A portly man wearing a flowered shirt stood beside a boat, posing proudly beside a strung-up shark so his wife could snap pictures. Gulls wheeled overhead or pestered passersby for morsels of food.

Bolan strolled along the docks until he came to the boat he wanted. It was a newer powerboat rigged with a tuna tower and a high platform. Outriggers jutted high into the air at the stern.

Seated in the fighting chair, sipping a beer, was a bronzed man in shorts and sandals. His profile revealed Spanish blood in his family tree. A mane of black hair and bushy black eyebrows lent him the appearance of a jungle wildman. About to take another swallow, he noticed Bolan and grinned. "*Hola, señor.* You are late."

"Some last-minute business came up," Bolan said, stepping over the gunwale onto the cockpit. He set his duffel near the freezer.

Ramon Munoz glanced sharply at the long green bag. "You are all set, then, I take it?"

"As ready as I'll ever be," Bolan said good-naturedly. "How long will it take us to get there?"

Munoz rose and quaffed the last of his brew. "An hour or so. It is hard to find at night, and I have been there only once before, you know."

"So you told me. I'm just glad I found someone who will take me. Every other charter-boat operator refused."

"Ah, well. You know how it is," Munoz said, moving to cast off the line. "Men of the sea are very superstitious, and Dominique Island has a very bad reputation. It is claimed that the waters around it are filled with reefs and thick with sharks. So no one goes anywhere near it."

"Doesn't that worry you?" Bolan asked.

"For enough money, Señor Belasko, I will do just about anything. And you are paying a lot of money to go there."

"Belasko" was the alias Bolan was using at the moment. He followed the boat owner up the ladder to the flying bridge and sat in the bench seat while Munoz devoted his attention to the control console.

"Now that I think of it, *señor,*" Munoz asked casually, "you haven't told me why you want to. Maybe it would be wise to let me know, eh, in case you expect trouble."

"I work for the federal government," Bolan replied.

Munoz spun, fleeting fear etched on his face. "You do?"

"Yes. I'm taking a census of all the islands in the Florida Keys."

"A census?" Munoz repeated, his brow puckered. It took a full five seconds for him to understand, then he laughed in relief. "Oh! I get it! You count all the islands!" He slapped his leg as if it were the funniest thing he had ever heard. "You have a good sense of humor, *señor*. And I will take the hint. Ramon Munoz does not pry into matters that do not concern him."

"So I was told," Bolan said, thinking also of the great many other tidbits of information that had led him to the *Maria* and the boat's black-haired owner.

Munoz opened a cooler that sat beside the console and helped himself to another beer. He offered a bottle to Bolan. "The nectar of the gods. I always keep plenty on hand."

"No, thanks."

The engine chugged to life. Propeller wash churned the water behind them as the *Maria* eased from her berth and made for open water. Munoz waved to a burly man operating an incoming craft, then he opened the throttle and the boat leaped forward.

The salty tang of sea water tingled Bolan's nostrils. He inhaled deeply, the wind whipping his hair. Off to port a pair of small fish playfully leaped out of the water and splashed down again. A few gulls circled above them, expecting handouts.

"This is the life, is it not?" Munoz asked. "The sea, the sun and all a man can eat if he but dips a hook in the water. What more could anyone ask for, *señor?*"

Bolan leaned back and draped his arms over the

back of the seat. Putting up with Munoz's chatter for two hours was the price he had to pay to check out his best lead to date.

According to a bartender who loved money almost as much as the charter operator did, it was rumored among the criminal element of Key West that Dominique Island figured prominently in Santoro's drug operation. No one could say exactly how. But several sources had warned Bolan that anyone who went near the island courted death.

Munoz turned on the radio and tuned it to a station playing Spanish pop music. He hummed along with the tune, rapping his hands on the wheel in time to the beat.

That morning, Bolan had phoned Hal Brognola and requested a background check on Munoz. Records indicated the man had lived in southern Florida his entire life and had a record as long as his arm. The arrests had always been for petty crimes: theft, burglary, drunk and disorderly. But three years earlier Munoz had moved to Key West and hadn't had a blemish on his record since. The man had either gone straight or he was making a special effort not to draw any attention to himself.

Munoz was feeling talkative. "Did you know that back in the old days, *señor*, these waters were home to many pirates? Every now and then someone finds one of their sunken ships, sometimes with treasure still on board." He hungrily surveyed the Gulf of Mexico. "I would love to find one of them."

"What would you do if you did?" Bolan said to make conversation.

"Surely you joke again." Munoz smacked his lips like a man offered a gourmet feast. "I would move to South America and set myself up like a king in Chile, Bolivia or perhaps Brazil. Pretty *señoritas* would wait on me day and night. I would drive the best of cars and wear the best of clothes. It would be heaven."

"Ever been to South America?"

"*Sí, señor.* I have visited Colombia three times—" Munoz caught himself and gave the soldier a peculiar look. "Why do you ask?"

Bolan shrugged. "No real reason." He paused. "If you've been to Colombia that many times, why not settle there? I hear it's a nice country."

"To visit, maybe. But surely you have heard of all the killing that goes on there? Drug lords do as they please. Many of the police are little better than thugs. And right-wing death squads can strike at any time." Munoz gestured. "No, I would take my millions and live where there is law and order."

This from a man once arrested for assaulting a police officer who was citing him for speeding. Bolan found it interesting that Munoz had been to Colombia. In itself, the admission meant little. But in light of the influx of coke, it established a possible link to the cartels.

Bolan had been waging war against the Colombian drug lords for years. Again and again he would cripple their operations. Again and again they recovered and rerouted their pipelines into the U.S.

Sometimes it seemed to Bolan that for every two steps forward he took, he also took three steps back.

But he wouldn't let himself grow discouraged. To win the good war, he had to persevere. It wasn't how many drug operations he crushed or how many drug lords he terminated—it was knowing that every time he put a crimp in their operations, he slowed the flow of drugs into America. Even if that only meant one less addict hooked a month, or one less schoolkid pressured into being a dealer, it made the battle worthwhile.

Munoz consulted a map and changed course, bearing eastward.

Dominique Island was located far off the beaten path, as it were, so far out of the normal sea lanes that rarely did anyone pass by, superstition or not. Bolan had researched it well. He knew the island was near the boundary of the Great White Heron refuge. It was small, less than two acres in extent, shaped similar to a teardrop, and could only be approached from the north because of the reefs.

The sea soon swallowed the sun. Twilight lent the gulf a strange glow that dimmed as the stars increased. Before too long the *Maria* was operating by instruments alone, her powerful twin engines purring like contented kittens.

Saying he needed to stretch his legs, Bolan went down the ladder and paced the cockpit awhile, then took a seat in the fighting chair.

In reality, he wanted to learn if they were being followed. If all had gone well, José Santoro knew that he had chartered the boat. Sooner or later Santoro would make another attempt on his life.

Twenty minutes of close scrutiny turned up no

trace of another craft, but Bolan wasn't about to take it for granted that no one was back there. Any boat with a radar unit could stay well out of sight and still dog them to their destination.

True to Munoz's word, one hour and four minutes after leaving Key West, he cut back on the throttle and announced, "We are very close, Señor Belasko."

Bolan climbed back up to the flying bridge. The boat owner was peering intently into the darkness ahead. "How close exactly?"

Munoz activated a spotlight that knifed through the night like a lighthouse beacon. Dimly, at the limits of its glare, an enormous murky shape materialized. "Does that answer your question?" He swung the wheel hard to bring the *Maria* around to the north. "We might be too near. Keep watch for reefs, *por favor.*"

Bolan stepped to the safety rail and scanned the water as Munoz played the spotlight over it. A dark mass took form nearby. "There's one to starboard," Bolan warned, pointing.

"Gracias."

Munoz reduced speed to a crawl and swung to port, narrowly missing the reef.

It was plain that Munoz had miscalculated. They should have swung north well before he did, and now they were in very real danger of punching a hole in the hull and being shipwrecked.

Another reef loomed, to port this time. Munoz spun the wheel like a madman. Both of them heard a grating creak, and Bolan leaned over the side to see better. A coral spine rubbed against the hull, scraping paint but not gouging deep enough to break through. "Nice and easy," he advised.

Munoz was pale. "You do not need to tell me twice," he said, handling the wheel now as if it were as delicate as fine china. He swore a few times, then added, "I knew I should have asked you for more money. If I wreck here, the insurance company might not pay up."

"We'll make it," Bolan said to bolster the man's confidence. The last thing they needed was a nervous wreck at the helm.

The *Maria* safely passed the reef and threaded around several more. After they had gone several hundred feet and not seen any others, Munoz turned due east. Traveling only a short distance, he brought the boat around to a southerly heading.

Bolan relaxed a little. They were closing on the island from the north, as originally intended. He moved close to the console. "Rove your light over the shore."

Munoz complied. The beam revealed a rocky strip bordered by dense vegetation.

Bolan was mildly surprised. It looked like a jungle in there, and he had been expecting a flat, barren spine of rock. So much the better. The jungle, after all, was his element. His lethal skills had been honed in the sweltering jungles of Vietnam.

"What now, *señor?*" Munoz asked. "You only say to bring you here. What next?"

Bolan nodded at the shore. "Drop me off and leave. Come back in three days to pick me up."

Munoz was astounded, and it showed. "You can't

be serious. This island is a bad place. Many snakes and bugs live here.''

"How would you know?" Bolan responded. "I thought you said that you've never been on it?"

The wily boat operator bobbed his shoulders. "Ah, well. I talk to men who have been. There is no water to drink, little to eat. You would starve in three days. So why not go back with me and forget this silly idea of yours?"

Bolan started down the ladder. "Just take us in as close as you can." Dropping from the third rung, he moved to the transom and leaned on the gunwale. No lights showed other than the myriad of sparkling stars. He mentally crossed his fingers that Santoro had taken the bait, or he was back at square one with no other solid leads.

Munoz swung the *Maria* around and inched toward the shore in reverse. There weren't supposed to be any reefs on that side of the island, but he was taking no chances. When only about six feet out, he killed the engine and quickly let down the anchor. "I will help you go ashore, *señor*," he announced.

"That's not necessary."

"I insist." Munoz whisked down the ladder by gripping the side rails and sliding. Smiling broadly, he scooted to the duffel and grabbed the carrying strap with one hand. "Since you chartered my boat, I am responsible for you, eh? I must make sure you do not get hurt."

"I can take care of myself," Bolan insisted.

Munoz started to lift the duffel but jerked up short. "*¡Caramba!* What do you have in here? It must weigh a ton." Taking hold with both hands, he hoisted the duffel bag as high as his chest and walked slowly toward the soldier. "You must be strong, amigo. I saw you carrying it with one arm."

Bolan anticipated an attempt on his life. The way he had it figured, Munoz was the one who had alerted Santoro to his presence in Key West. According to the bartender with the loose lips, Munoz was rumored to haul drugs for Santoro on occasion. And Dominique Island was a pickup point.

The Executioner had counted on Munoz going to his boss when a strange man showed up and asked to be taken to the island the next evening. He'd had high hopes that it would flush Santoro into the open. Instead, Santoro had sicced Baker and Sammy on him.

Now, as Munoz crossed the cockpit, Bolan tensed, ready for any eventuality. Or so he thought. Braced as he was, he still couldn't prevent Munoz from suddenly hurling the heavy duffel at him. Nor could he skip aside in time to avoid it. The duffel hit him in the ribs and sent him sprawling against the transom. Before he could rise, Munoz was on him, a butterfly knife flashing dully in the starlight.

The blade streaked at Bolan's throat, but he dropped under it and kicked, knocking Munoz backward. It gave the soldier the room he needed to spring to his feet and grab for the Beretta. His fingers were closing on the butt when Munoz shrieked and rushed madly at him, swinging the butterfly knife in a frenzy. Only by the sheerest luck was Bolan able to seize the man's knife arm.

Munoz made no attempt to stop. He plowed into the soldier like a runaway Brahman bull, his momentum sweeping them both against the gunwale, and over it.

Bolan dared not let go of Munoz's arm. Locked together, they pitched into the water. A cold, clammy sheath enveloped him, the salt stinging his eyes.

The water was only waist deep. Bolan surged erect, hauling Munoz up with him. The man rained punches with his free hand. One clipped Bolan's cheek, and another grazed his temple.

Struggling fiercely, the two men twisted and turned, neither able to gain a decided edge. There was no science to Munoz's assault. He was no boxer or martial artist. He fought with desperation, seeking to overpower his adversary through sheer ferocity. It made him all the more dangerous.

Slick rocks were underfoot. Suddenly Bolan slipped on one and nearly went under again. Munoz applied all his strength, striving to drive the butterfly knife into Bolan's throat. The soldier locked both hands on his adversary's arm to keep the blade at bay.

Eyes glittering like those of a rabid wolf, Munoz grabbed Bolan by the collar and wrenched, forcing him to lose his balance. Water poured into his mouth, into his nose, and for a few seconds he couldn't see his foe although he did keep his grip on the knife arm.

A stinging sensation racked Bolan's left shoulder as he shot to his feet. He had been wrong. In the brief instant he had been under, Munoz had switched the butterfly from one hand to the other. The keen blade had nicked Bolan, the injury minor only because Munoz hadn't taken the time to set himself before striking.

Spinning, Bolan performed a flawless judo flip that sent Munoz sailing head over heels. The thug crashed onto his back in the bubbling surf at land's edge and rose shakily.

Bolan waded in. He was almost within arm's reach when Munoz skipped to the left, dashed across the rocky strip and paused at the verdant wall of vegetation.

"We will get you yet, gringo! You will see!" With that, Munoz plunged into the undergrowth.

The soldier took a few steps after him, then thought better of the idea. Drawing the Beretta, he backed out to the boat and clambered aboard. Munoz had outsmarted himself. Now Bolan could do with the *Maria* as he pleased.

Squatting beside the duffel, Bolan opened it. First he took out his holstered Desert Eagle and strapped it to his right thigh. Next he removed his M-16, which he had broken down into the upper and lower receiver groups for storage.

Working swiftly, Bolan reassembled the rifle. Slapping in a 30-round magazine, he leaned the rifle against his leg and rummaged in the duffel for a few other lethal tools of his trade. He also strapped a Ka-bar fighting knife above his right ankle. Securing the duffel again, he rose.

Mocking laughter wafted from the island. Bolan brought up the M-16 but could see nothing beyond the black wall of growth. So far as he knew, the only weapon Munoz had was the knife. But if the smugglers were using Dominique Island on a regular basis, there might be a cache of supplies and weapons. He had to stay frosty.

Bolan climbed to the flying bridge. As he stepped to the console, more laughter taunted him. Munoz seemed to be enjoying himself immensely.

"Go ahead, *señor!* Try to start her! You are not going anywhere!"

Bolan did. He wanted to lay offshore a short distance and wait to see if another boat showed up. But the *Maria* wouldn't turn over. Every time he tried, he heard a muted click. "An override relay," he said to himself. It was another smuggler trick, a circuit rigged to prevent anyone from making off with contraband. There had to be a trigger or button somewhere on the bridge, but finding it might take an hour or more and Bolan didn't know how much time he had to spare.

"What did I tell you?" Munoz gloated. "Maybe you should get out and push!"

Bolan gripped the spotlight control and swung the beam landward. It splashed over the foliage from right to left. Other than a brief hint of movement, there was no sign of the boat's devious owner. Bolan kept the light trained on the general area where he believed Munoz to be, then went below.

Shouldering the duffel, Bolan slipped over the side and carefully worked his way to the left. If all went well, the blinding glare of the spotlight would keep Munoz from spotting him before he gained cover.

Fortunately the night was warm and muggy. Although Bolan was soaked to the skin, he wasn't cold. Reaching dry ground, he crouched, surveyed the strip of beach, then darted into a gap in the trees. He leaned against a smooth trunk to listen. Normally insects would be droning, frogs croaking. But the island was as silent as a tomb. With one exception.

"Peekaboo! I saw you!" Munoz yelled from off to the west. "You think that you are clever, but you are not!"

Bolan went deeper, seeking a spot to make his stand. The growth was so thick that he wished he'd brought a machete.

"Did you hear me, Señor Belasko, or whatever your real name is?" Munoz called out. "Make your peace with your Maker, my friend, because you are not long for this world. You wanted to get your hands on José Santoro, but he has turned the tables. Even now the jaws of his trap are closing. Soon you will be a dead man. Very soon indeed!"

3

The Executioner didn't like the sound of that. Munoz was much too sure of himself. He wondered if Santoro already had men waiting on the island. Adopting a combat crouch, he snaked inland, senses primed. He rotated the selector lever on the M-16 from auto to semi. Discriminate fire was called for, not spraying the jungle at random.

Munoz had stopped talking. A twig snapped in his general direction.

Bolan brought up the rifle but couldn't pinpoint the smuggler. Veering eastward, he came to a patch of high weeds. He eased onto his belly and crawled, rustling the stems as little as possible. Suddenly a trail opened up before him, running from north to south. He stopped and looked both ways.

A loud splash came from the vicinity of the *Maria* and Bolan guessed that Munoz had gone back out to the boat. He began to rise, then froze as something slithered onto his right leg. Ever so slowly, the soldier looked over his shoulder.

It was a big snake, and it stopped and reared its head, sensing his movement. In the dark all Bolan could see was the black outline of its sinuous form and the darting of its forked tongue as it turned its head from side to side, testing the air.

Bolan had no idea what kind of snake it might be. He did know that the Keys were home to coral snakes and cottonmouths and other dangerous species. There had even been rumors recently of cobras gaining a foothold in south Florida, thanks to pet owners foolish enough to release full-grown specimens into the wild when their pets were no longer wanted.

Whatever this one was, it hissed angrily and slid a few inches higher on Bolan's leg. In the pale starlight its slanted eyes had a demonic quality, seemingly lit with an inner fire. The snake swayed, then dipped toward Bolan's shoulder. He tensed involuntarily for the bite he was sure would be inflicted. But the serpent apparently considered him harmless, because it abruptly turned and crawled off, vanishing in the high grass.

Bolan glided south along the trail. Traveling thirty yards, he stopped under a large tree, a thick trunk leading up to long, gnarled branches. An ideal vantage point, Bolan reflected, setting down the duffel. Slipping the M-16's sling over his left shoulder, he shinned up to the lowest limb, gripped it and swung higher, moving from branch to branch until he was a good thirty feet above the ground.

Right away Bolan discovered more than he had bargained for. Another fishing boat was anchored near the *Maria*. Vague figures bustled about. On the flying bridge of the newcomer stood a squat figure growling orders right and left. It had to be Santoro.

As the soldier looked on, half a dozen men clad in black dropped off the back of Santoro's craft and waded to shore. Fanning out, they blended into the vegetation.

Bolan's plan had worked a little too well. Granted, he had flushed Santoro out of hiding, but now he was up against a hit squad of six pros armed with automatic weapons. Even worse, the six had probably been to the island before and were familiar with the terrain. He wasn't.

Dropping from limb to limb, Bolan let himself fall the last six feet and landed lightly on the balls of his feet. Retrieving the duffel, he turned and jogged to the south. The trail had to lead somewhere, and he was curious to find out exactly where. In another hundred yards a clearing broadened before him.

Bolan had unslung the M-16 along the way. Swiveling the barrel from side to side, he stalked toward a small hut. Beside it was a peculiar mound, and closer inspection revealed the mound to be a waterproof tarp draped over four crates. Sliding a pencil flashlight from a pocket, he discovered that three of the crates contained ammunition, the fourth food rations.

The shack was a crude structure made of warped planks and old two-by-fours. There was no door, per se, just a blanket that had been nailed across a narrow opening. Bolan shoved the blanket aside with the rifle and roved his beam over the interior.

It was a hovel. A battered cot lined one flimsy wall, and an ancient kerosene stove roosted in a rear corner. Empty, discarded tin cans, whiskey bottles and crushed beer cans littered the earthen floor. So did decayed chicken bones. The place reeked.

A layer of dust told Bolan that the shack hadn't been used in ages. Evidently it was there in case any of the smugglers had to stay on the island for any length of time, which they rarely did.

Bolan dug into a pants pocket and withdrew an M-67 fragmentation grenade. From another pocket he pulled a short roll of thin wire. Kneeling, he scooped a small hole just inside the doorway, on the left, and wedged the grenade into the hole. Then, slipping the end of the wire through the pull ring on the safety pin, he tied it securely, strung the wire across the entrance at ankle height and looped it around the head of a nail. His Ka-bar knife sufficed to snip the wire.

Off in the woods a bird erupted in agitated squawks. Something, or someone, had disturbed its rest.

The soldier hurried into heavy brush to the east. Once safe from prying eyes, he searched for a suitable spot to stash the duffel. The hollow stump of a tree offered a perfect hiding place.

Bolan continued eastward until the shore appeared through the trees. It was more sandy than the north beach and ringed by breakers thirty yards out.

No boats were visible, and he deemed it safe to emerge from cover. Hugging the tree line, he trotted northward again, circling the island to return to where the *Maria* and the other boat were bobbing gently on the water. As he came around the northeast point, he slowed and stayed as low to the ground as he could.

Santoro and company were overconfident. Spotlights illuminated the scene as brightly as day, revealing Santoro still on the flying bridge, with Munoz. Two gunners were on hand to protect them in the cockpit of Santoro's craft. Another pair was on shore.

No one was on the *Maria*.

Bolan flattened and crept to the water's edge. Holding the M-16 so it would not get wet, he slid in, coiled his legs under him and angled toward the *Maria*'s starboard bow. Only his face and the rifle were above the surface.

The footing was just as treacherous as it had been earlier, the slick rocks threatening to spill him into the water every few feet. He placed each foot down slowly and didn't move on until confident he had solid purchase.

The four gunners were intent on the vegetation. They didn't expect any trouble from the sea. Santoro appeared unhappy with Munoz and kept jabbing his underling in the chest.

Gradually the water deepened. As it did, Bolan straightened his legs just enough to compensate. He was still forty feet from the side deck when the sea bottom slanted steeply downward. Pausing, he tried to gauge exactly how deep it was by probing with his left foot. Plainly the only way he would reach the bow was by swimming.

Pushing off from the edge of the drop-off, Bolan slowly swam forward, hoping the now wet assault rifle would perform when called upon. He made no noise whatsoever, and the few ripples he created weren't big enough to draw attention. The voices of Santoro and Munoz drifted his way on the stiff breeze. Santoro was doing most of the talking, in Spanish. Bolan had a good grounding in the language and was able to follow most of the conversation.

"I should gut you and throw your worthless carcass to the sharks, Ramon! You should have killed him, like I wanted you to do."

"I tried," Munoz whined. "But he is a devil. Very fast and immensely strong. I was lucky he did not kill me, like he did Baker and Sammy."

"Those two were morons. I was told they were the best Key West had to offer. If so, I will import talent from now on."

"Why bother? You have more than enough men here to handle the Fed," Munoz said smugly.

As if to prove him wrong, the jungle rocked with an explosion. An undulating scream rose to a piercing pitch before strangling off into a mournful groan.

"There!" Munoz exclaimed. "Your men have taken care of him."

"Stupid!" Santoro fumed. "My men did not have grenades!" He commenced snarling orders.

By then Bolan was clinging to the rub rail of the *Maria*. The spotlights were all pointed inland, so he was able to pull himself onto the foredeck in near total darkness. Worming aft along the starboard rail, he was almost to the tuna tower when there was a loud thud and the *Maria* rolled, as if over a swell.

Munoz had jumped into the cockpit from the deck

of the other fishing boat. Muttering, he scampered up the ladder to the bridge. "I will follow you out, Chief!" he hollered.

Bolan was in the open with nowhere to hide. If Munoz glanced over the rail, he would lose the element of surprise. But the smuggler proved too busy hoisting the anchor and preparing to get under way to notice him. Bolan crawled as far as the outrigger. Silently rising, he held on to the pole and peeked out over the cockpit.

The two gunners who had been on shore were back in the other boat, which was heading out to sea.

Santoro, Bolan deduced, was worried about having a grenade lobbed onto his craft. His hunch proved right when the smugglers traveled only fifty or sixty feet and stopped.

Munoz muttered the entire time. He coasted the *Maria* the final few yards and brought it in close to Santoro's boat. Once the engines had been killed again, he stepped to the port side and said, "How soon before the shipment gets here, if I may ask?"

"In a rush to see that whore of yours?" Santoro responded.

Angered by the remark, Munoz said testily, "Maria is no prostitute!"

"Oh. Excuse me. I thought that is what you call a woman who goes to bed with men for money. How stupid I am. She must be a nun." Santoro chortled wickedly.

Bolan marked the position of the four gunners. It was time to make his move. If all went well, he would take out the triggerman but only wing Santoro.

There were questions that only the leader of the ring could answer.

At that moment, fate dealt the soldier a bad hand. Two men in black appeared on the shore, and the taller one shouted across the water. "Mr. Santoro! We've lost Rafe and Tony! They tripped a grenade!"

Santoro moved to the top of the ladder. "That is what happens when a man is careless, Brewster! Get back in there and see that you do not make the same mistake they did! And do not take all night about it."

Bolan saw Brewster begin to turn. The hardman glanced at the *Maria* and seemed to do a double take. Bolan knew, even before the man yelled, that the situation had just gone critical.

"Mr. Santoro! I think someone is hanging on the side of Munoz's boat!"

The Executioner was in motion before the last words were out of Brewster's mouth. Leaping, he grabbed the gin pole and swung onto the cockpit near the fighting chair. As he landed, he whipped the M-16 from his shoulder, pivoted and triggered three rounds at a gunner on Santoro's boat. The man dropped like a puppet with its strings severed. Pivoting, Bolan sighted on a second gunner and cored the man's head.

Belatedly the rest were galvanized to life. The pair in the cockpit of the other boat and the pair on shore all cut loose at the same time.

Bolan hit the deck, as a swarm of lead hornets buzzed overhead. Slugs bit into the transom and ripped into the fighting chair and the sliding door that fronted the cockpit. Above him, Munoz screamed in rage as his beloved boat was chewed up.

The shooters made the same mistake that so many of their kind had made in the past. In their zeal to kill their enemy, they emptied their magazines into the fishing boat.

Bolan was ready. Switching the M-16 to autofire, he pushed to his knees the second the firing stopped and sprayed the shore with a short burst. His rounds stitched holes in both Brewster and his companion, and they danced backward as if doing a jig before collapsing into heaps. Swiveling, Bolan saw the gunners in the back of Santoro's boat frantically trying to shove new magazines into their SMGs. They were a shade too slow. His M-16 chopped them off at the waist.

The Executioner dashed to the port gunwale and elevated the rifle, but there was no sign of Santoro. He couldn't let the leader escape. Raising a foot onto the gunwale to spring onto the other craft, he stiffened as a scream of raw fury rent the night, and he glanced up at the *Maria*'s flying bridge.

Munoz was in midair, the glittering butterfly knife clenched in his right hand. Like a vengeful bird of prey, he swooped on top of the Executioner. Bolan barely swept up the M-16 in time to parry the blade. The impact bowled him over into the water. Munoz fell with him, on top, slashing repeatedly at Bolan's face and neck. As they went under, the soldier flipped to the right, throwing the smuggler off. They shot erect at the same moment. Bolan palmed the Ka-bar fighting knife as he straightened so that when

Munoz pounced once more, he was ready, slicing the knife to the hilt into Munoz's chest.

Wailing in pain, Munoz clutched at the knife, tripped over his own feet and fell. He made no attempt to get up, dead before he sank under the surface.

Bolan promptly became aware of two new elements. The twin engines on Santoro's boat coughed and sputtered, flooded by the smuggler's frenetic attempts to gun them. And on the shore, the last two triggermen had materialized and were rushing to their boss's aid.

Miniature geysers shot into the air on either side of Bolan as the hardmen closed in. He flung himself against the *Maria* so the aft corner would shield him from their withering fire. In a span of heartbeats, they tapered off. Popping into the open, Bolan unleashed a sustained burst.

The gunners had no cover. They were less than twenty feet away, up to their knees in the water. One snapped off several shots just as his face dissolved in a spray of scarlet. The other henchman had his torso peppered.

At last Bolan could concentrate on nabbing José Santoro. But as he turned, the other craft, which had the word *Sisto* painted on its transom, rumbled to life. Bolan took two swift strides and lunged, his outflung hand missing the vessel's gunwale by a hair as the boat shot forward, its wash spewing around him.

Santoro looked back and grinned wolfishly. Jabbing a hand into the air, he extended his middle finger.

Bolan didn't waste a second. He was on the *Maria* and flying up the ladder before the *Sisto* had gone twenty yards. His only hope was that Munoz hadn't activated the override relay after moving the fishing boat farther out. If he had to search for the switch, Santoro would get away.

The engines turned right over. Bolan threw the twin throttles open wide and swerved toward the wake of the *Sisto*. He disliked leaving his duffel behind, but he could always come back for it later.

The drug smuggler was pushing his craft to its limit, looping to the west to skirt the reefs.

Thanks to the stiff wind, choppy waves bounced the two boats like bobbers. Placing the M-16 on the console in front of him, Bolan brushed spray from his brow and tried his best to overtake Santoro.

It soon became apparent that the two craft were powered by near equal horsepower. Even holding the throttles all the way open, Bolan couldn't gain ground. He had about resigned himself to a long chase when the smuggler did a peculiar thing.

Suddenly the *Sisto* slowed. Santoro held what appeared to be a radio in his right hand and was gesturing furiously at the *Maria*.

Puzzled, Bolan also reduced speed a little. Santoro was clearly in contact with someone else, maybe another boat nearby. The soldier scanned the sea but saw no evidence of one. All he noticed was the hump of a large reef off to the northwest, barely visible.

As Bolan looked on, the reef moved.

His gaze narrowed. For a few seconds he thought that his eyes were playing tricks on him. But no, when he looked closer, he could see a mild disturbance in front of the object as it glided toward the *Maria*.

A gloating cackle fluttered across the water. Santoro had come to a complete stop and was leaning on the rear rail, watching.

Years of combat had honed Mack Bolan's senses to a degree few men possessed. He had an inner sixth sense, a sort of internal alarm that had saved his life on more occasions than he cared to count. Now that alarm flared again. A tiny voice deep within him urged that he get out of there, that he take evasive action and do it quickly.

Bolan acted on the warning instantly. Spinning the wheel, he powered up the boat and sped to the southwest, aware that he was putting himself dangerously close to the reefs but also certain that whatever was after him was far more deadly.

The object had increased its speed and was closing rapidly, but it was still too far away for him to see clearly.

On an impulse, Bolan cut sharply to the right, then to the left. His aim was to adopt a zigzag pattern in case the thing in the water turned out to be what he suspected it had to be.

Without warning, materializing out of the night, a much smaller object shot past the *Maria*'s stern, churning the water into a froth. It made no noise that Bolan could hear above the rumble of the vessel's engines. It didn't have to. He knew what it was, and he spun the wheel to the right to put as much distance between it and him as he could before the inevitable happened.

The fishing boat responded superbly. Bolan, hunched over the console, glanced back just as a shattering blast punctured the darkness. A reef had been hit and blown sky high.

Bolan shifted, seeking the source. In taking evasive action, he had lost sight of the mystery vessel. Now it appeared to be gone, but he knew better. It had submerged and was undoubtedly closing on him at a new angle, getting in as close as it could before launching another torpedo.

That was when Bolan noted something else. In swinging to the right, he had placed himself on a collision course with the *Sisto*.

Santoro was talking into the radio again, apparently advising his cohorts.

Bolan had an idea. Whoever had tried to blow him out of the water probably wouldn't try again if Santoro was at risk. The soldier drastically reduced speed and brought the *Maria* alongside the other vessel in a smooth arc. A loud grating sound signified that he couldn't get any closer without caving in both hulls.

Santoro, still on the radio, spun in alarm.

Throwing the control into neutral, Bolan took a short run, sprang onto the side rail and vaulted into space. For a harrowing moment it seemed he would fall short. Then his feet came down on the *Sisto*'s handrail even as he clutched at the top of the flying bridge and levered himself up and over.

By the helm seat, Santoro lowered the radio to grab at a pistol strapped to his right hip. Bolan's legs smashed him across the chest, slamming the smuggler into the seat, then over it. Santoro landed on his hands and knees. Snarling like a cornered panther, he spun, trying once more for the pistol. He almost had it out when Bolan's right foot impacted with his chin, felling him on the spot.

The soldier tore the handgun from the smuggler's fingers and tossed it over the side. Wrenching Santoro's right arm behind the man's back, he seized his thatch of dark hair and demanded, "Call them off!"

Santoro was groggy from the kick. Shaking his head to clear it, he attempted to twist, but Bolan held him in a steel vise. "You are a fool, gringo! Let me go while you have the chance. I can make it worth your while. How would you like more money than you can earn in a lifetime?"

"Call them off!" the soldier repeated.

"Why bother?" Santoro growled. "They won't do anything so long as you hold me!"

Bolan glanced over the water. At the limit of his vision, something moved just under the surface, shooting like a rocket toward the two fishing boats. At the same moment, the smuggler saw it and cried out.

"No! What are they doing? I would never talk! They know that!"

Bolan's hunch had been wrong. Apparently the crew of the mini-submarine considered Santoro expendable. They had fired another torpedo.

4

The human mind is a marvelous instrument. It is the envy of every computer designer from Silicon Valley to Tokyo. For no matter how fast computers can perform, no matter how many megabytes of memory they can boast, no computer ever made can match the intricacy and swiftness of the human mind.

In the split second that the Executioner set eyes on the incoming torpedo, he realized three options were open to him. He could let go of Santoro and dive over the side, but if both boats were destroyed in the blast, he'd end up stranded in the middle of nowhere with slim hope of ever being picked up by a passing craft. Or he could try to get the *Sisto* out of there before the torpedo struck. The only problem was that the *Sisto* had already flooded once when gunned. If it did so now, there wouldn't be enough pieces of him left for Brognola to find with a strainer. The third option was to leap back onto the *Maria* and bury the throttle.

All of this flashed through Bolan's mind in the span of several heartbeats. He picked the one possibility that offered the highest odds of survival.

Giving the smuggler a shove, Bolan raced to the end of the bridge and hurtled over the side. He pushed off unevenly and paid the price. His left leg swept out from under him as he alighted and he was thrown forward by his own momentum. By a fluke, he stumbled into the wheel, catching hold to steady himself. A flick of his wrist, and the *Maria* surged to life, racing northward.

Santoro had a hand on the *Sisto*'s throttle. He pushed it as far as it would go, but instead of speeding off, the boat sputtered and lurched, the fuel-intake valves once again drowned in diesel.

Like a squat metallic arrow, the torpedo cleaved the water, bearing down on the vessel. Santoro glanced at it and yelled in impotent rage.

Bolan saw the drug smuggler pound on the throttle, saw him whirl and take a step toward the port side of the fishing boat. The man never made it. A rending, splintering crash heralded the explosion. The stern of the *Sisto* tilted steeply out of the water. Twin explosions thundered across the gulf as the fuel went up. A fiery fist pulverized the vessel, leaving charred timbers and blistered fragments to rain to the water's surface.

The Executioner sped to the southwest. The sub was bound to give chase. Whether the souped-up fishing boat could outrace it was a moot point. The *Maria* certainly couldn't outrun a torpedo if the sub got close enough.

For tense minutes Bolan knifed across the sea, casting repeated looks behind him. A sticklike object broke the surface near the blazing remains of the *Sisto,* and circled. It was a periscope. A gleam on the lens from the moonlight told Bolan when it turned toward him. He shut off his running lights, then changed course to the south.

In a fine spray, the periscope bubbled under the surface.

The soldier felt like a proverbial sitting duck. Only when the lights of other boats confirmed Bolan was nearing Key West did he reduce speed and allow himself the luxury of relaxing. He would go back for the duffel the next day. For now, he had to contact Hal Brognola and tell the big Fed that they were up against a threat the likes of which they had never encountered before—minisubmarines.

"I KNOW," Brognola said calmly at the other end of the line. "A Coast Guard patrol boat out of the Alameda Coast Guard Base was sunk by one while on routine patrol a couple of nights ago. There were witnesses. An eighteen-year-old youth and his girlfriend were parked on a bluff overlooking the cove where it happened and saw the whole thing."

Bolan was in his hotel room in Key West, reclining on his bed with his back to the headboard. "There's another one operating off of California? What are we dealing with here? An entire fleet?"

"That's what the Man would like us to find out," Brognola said. "I don't need to tell you the stir this is causing in the White House. It escalates the drug war to a whole new level." He paused. "This takes top priority, Striker. We have to find out where these subs are being built, how they're slipping into our waters and where they lay low when they're not making drug runs."

"That's a tall order," Bolan commented.

"Maybe it won't be as hard as it seems. Submarines don't come cheap. Even minisubs. It would take a well-financed organization like a cartel or else a drug lord with more millions than he knows what to do with to pull off an operation of this scope. The small fry just couldn't come up with that much money."

Bolan had to agree. "That narrows the field, all right, but it must leave at least two dozen suspects. Checking out each and every one will take time."

"We have another angle to pursue. Sub parts are specialty items. It's not as if a person can walk into a local hardware store and buy a stabilizer fin. My people are checking all the supply houses, and I have a friend in Brazil who's doing the same in his neck of the woods. It'll take time, but we'll track them down."

"What do I do in the meantime?" Bolan asked.

"I've got something that should be a nice change of pace for you."

"Don't keep me in suspense."

"Let me put it this way. When was the last time you went hunting for sea serpents?"

THE INCIDENT had happened more than three weeks earlier. The story made national headlines only because it gave everyone a good laugh.

Two young and affluent couples from Brooklyn had bought yachts and decided to go on a long cruise. They had sailed down the Atlantic Seaboard, stopping wherever the whim struck. After passing through Florida Bay, they headed north for St. Petersburg, hugging the state's western shoreline.

It was near Naples that disaster struck.

One of the yachtsmen happened to glance out to sea near dusk and saw a freighter steaming north. Trailing it, he swore, was a genuine sea serpent. The man clearly saw its squat body and the silhouette of its serpentine neck. In his excitement, eager for a closer look, he abruptly changed course without a word of warning to his friends on the other yacht.

The resulting collision sank one yacht and severely damaged the other. It limped into port at Fort Myers, where the accident was reported to authorities. A leak to the media brought a horde of reporters down on the hapless couples.

Ordinarily Hal Brognola would never have given the news item a second thought. But the description of the so-called sea serpent, in light of recent developments, prompted him to go back and study the news reports again.

A check of shipping records revealed that three freighters had been in the general area at the time of the alleged sighting. One hailed from Mexico, another from Brazil, while the third flew a Honduran flag but was owned by a company in Colombia. That last tidbit of information was unearthed only after much effort on the part of Brognola's special investigative unit.

The Colombian tie fueled the big Fed's curiosity. He'd ordered a more thorough background check of the coastal freighter involved, the *Cartagena*. It turned out that the ship made two runs per month from Colombia to the United States. The cargo varied. But one pertinent fact never did, namely that the freighter passed Key West on each and every trip.

Bolan was in luck. The ship had arrived at St. Petersburg the day before and wouldn't be leaving for another thirty-six hours. He promptly chartered a private plane that flew him to the St. Petersburg–Clearwater International Airport. It was shortly after noon when he arrived. From the airport he took a taxi to a motel near the docks. Leaving his duffel, he went for a stroll.

It was a warm day, but Bolan wore a blue jacket and bought a seaman's cap in a used-clothing store on the way to the waterfront. With his shoulders hunched, the cap low and his collar pulled up, he mingled with the longshoremen bustling about the busy port.

The *Cartagena* wasn't hard to find. She was berthed third in a row of seven freighters. Nothing appeared out of the ordinary. Bolan observed a load of paper products being lowered into the hold.

As the soldier lingered by a stack of crates, he felt eyes on him. Looking up, he discovered a burly, unkempt man in a pea jacket studying him. As casually as possible, he strolled off, making it a point to watch the goings-on at other ships so it wouldn't appear he had singled out the *Cartagena* for special attention. When next he glanced back, the man in the pea jacket was gone.

The *Cartagena* was due to sail with the morning tide. Bolan found a pay phone at a tackle shop and contacted Brognola to find out if the Feds had been able to obtain a search warrant.

"I wish," Brognola said bitterly. "Lack of probable cause, is how the judge put it. We're dead in the water. Pardon the pun. I'm counting on you to get us the proof we need, Striker. Just be careful. If you get into trouble, you're on your own. I can't get a special unit there much before the ship sails."

"I prefer working alone anyway. You know that. I'll contact you later."

Since there wasn't much the soldier could do in broad daylight, he returned to the motel, set the clock-radio alarm for six that evening and indulged in an afternoon nap so he would be fresh and sharp later on. When the music blared, Bolan took a cold shower to jangle his nerves to life, helped himself to a cup of scalding black coffee from a vending machine in the lobby and emerged as twilight blanketed southern Florida.

The waterfront had quieted considerably. The day shift had called it quits, and the swing shift was just getting started. Few of the longshoremen the Executioner passed gave him a second look.

Bolan went past the *Cartagena* without so much as a sideways glance. Once a pallet of boxes screened him, though, he found a convenient crack and peered out to note the comings and goings of the crew.

The sky darkened, and streetlights flared to life up and down the waterfront. Out in the harbor, a tug blew its whistle.

Bolan was going to wait until after midnight to

make his move, when most of the crew would be asleep.

Just then the man in the pea jacket he'd seen earlier appeared, ambling down the gangplank with several husky sailors. On reaching the bottom, Pea Jacket took a cigar from a pocket and one of the others leaped to light it for him.

It had to be the captain, Bolan guessed. He stayed put until they were well on their way, then shadowed them, always staying well back.

The seamen walked to a bar appropriately named The Sea Shanty. Lusty laughter and tinny music belched through the open door as they filed in.

Pulling his cap down low, Bolan let a minute go by, then followed them. He stepped to the right so his back was to the wall and took stock. It was so dark that his eyes took a minute to adjust.

The place reeked of alcohol and smoke. On the left a bar ran the length of the room, while tables filled the middle. Along the near wall was a small empty stage. The music came from a jukebox in the corner.

A plump woman wearing a dress so skimpy that it should have been illegal approached Bolan and gave him the sort of look a rancher in the market for a new stud might give a splendid stallion.

"Well, hello handsome! Haven't seen you here before. My name is Polly. I own this place. Care for a table?" Her gaze raked him up and down again. "Or anything else?"

The crew from the *Cartagena* was already at a table across the room. "A beer at the bar will do,"

Bolan said, and walked by. He avoided gazing toward Pea Jacket. Sliding onto a stool at the end of the counter, he signaled the bartender and ordered a bottle.

The men from the freighter were in no great hurry. They ordered a meal and spent the next hour and a half eating and swapping tales.

Bolan nursed the beer for all it was worth. He was close enough to their table to overhear snatches of talk, most of which had to do with their ship, and women. Deciding it was time to sneak onto the *Cartagena* to look around, the Executioner started to rise but stopped on hearing a remark by a man at another table.

A tall sailor with a grizzled beard had turned in his chair to regard Pea Jacket. "Estabo, you son of a bitch! Where have you been keeping yourself? Out after sea serpents?"

Several men at both tables laughed, but Captain Estabo wasn't one of them. "I have more important things to do with my time, Telfar."

The owner, Polly, was passing with a tray of food expertly balanced in one hand. Stopping next to Estabo's table, she said, "What's this about a sea serpent?"

Telfar chortled. "Didn't you hear the news a few weeks back? Some idiot from New York rammed his yacht into another boat after he saw a sea serpent playing follow-the-leader with our friend's ship."

"Do tell," Polly said, and smiled at Estabo. "I never heard the *Cartagena* mentioned on the news."

"For a very good reason," Estabo said. "I refused

to be party to that nonsense. There was no sea beast. If there had been, a member of my crew would have seen it."

Telfar arched an eyebrow. "I seem to recall that one of your men did see something unusual once. About a year ago, remember? It was that young fellow from Argentina, the one who fell overboard and drowned."

"I had no idea your memory was so good," the captain said crisply. "But as you just pointed out, that took place over a year ago. There is no connection with the incident involving the yachts."

Telfar winked at his companions, then said, "No, that must have been a different sea serpent. If you ask me, your old scow must attract them like dead meat draws flies."

Estabo was on his feet in the blink of an eye, his right hand in the pocket of his pea jacket. "Insult my ship again and you will lose that sarcastic tongue of yours."

Polly quickly moved between their tables. "None of that, if you please! You boys know I don't tolerate any roughhousing in my place. If you want to fight, take it out in the back alley. Or better yet, down the street, so I don't have to hassle with the cops."

"Relax, both of you," Telfar said. "I was only poking fun. I meant no insult."

"Sure, you didn't," Estabo said flatly. Nodding curtly at his cronies, he stalked from the Sea Shanty, his men in tow.

Bolan stood to follow and overheard another interesting comment.

"That overbearing swine!" Telfar said loud enough for everyone in the bar to hear. "Mark my words! He'll get his one day. And if the rumors going around are true, it will be sooner than he thinks." The grizzled man smiled smugly. "The authorities might like to hear about all the strange goings-on on that ship of his."

"Hush!" Polly cautioned anxiously. "Are you so drunk that you can't think straight? It's not smart to talk like that, even in jest!"

"Who's joking?" Telfar retorted.

Bolan happened to glance toward the front of the building and discovered that the door was open a crack. It eased quietly shut, as if someone had been eavesdropping.

"I mean it, Eric," Polly said. "If word got back to Estabo, your life wouldn't be worth a dead herring."

"I'm not scared of that jackass," Telfar boasted. "I've licked better men than him with one arm tied behind my back." Polishing off the last of his whiskey, he rose, winked at Polly and strutted from the bar.

Bolan followed. The sailor had turned left and was strolling along without a care in the world, head bent, whistling loudly. So loudly that he never heard Bolan as the Executioner swiftly came up behind him.

Telfar came abreast of an alley. Taking two bounds, Bolan pounced, seizing the man by the scruff of the neck and the elbow. He propelled him a dozen feet into the alley and shoved him against a wall.

The seaman spun, a blade flashing dully in the

shadows. "Estabo, you scum—" he roared, and did a double take on seeing Bolan, who made no attempt to disarm him. "You're not Estabo. Who are you, and what's the big idea?"

"We have to talk," Bolan informed him.

"Talk, my ass!" Telfar said. "No one throws me around like I'm a sack of potatoes! Get out of my way, whoever you are, before I gut you!"

Bolan stayed where he was. Folding his arms across his chest, he said, "I get the impression that you're not very fond of Captain Estabo of the *Cartagena*."

Telfar cocked his head, examining Bolan as if he were an alien life-form. "It's no big secret," he answered. "But what's it to you? What is this all about?"

"You mentioned strange goings-on on Estabo's ship. I'd like to hear about them."

"Why do you want to know?" Telfar pressed him. "Who are you?"

Bolan offered no reply. Technically he had no formal status, no legal right to be questioning the sailor the way he was. He certainly couldn't claim he was working in conjunction with the U.S. Justice Department, since the official government line was that he didn't even exist.

Fortunately Bolan had no need to say a word. The sailor leaped to the same wrong conclusion the triggermen in Key West had made.

"You must be a Fed!" Telfar declared, lowering the switchblade a trifle. "Is that it? You're investigating what he's up to, I'll bet!"

"What can you tell me?" Bolan prompted.

Now that he knew he wasn't going to be harmed, Telfar's cocky attitude returned. Twirling the knife, he chuckled and responded, "A lot, mister. Believe me. But what's in it for me if I do? How much are you willing to pay?"

"Not one dime."

Telfar couldn't hide his chagrin. "That's a hell of a note. It should be worth a few hundred at least. What do you say? Slip me a few bills and I'll sing like a songbird."

Bolan sighed. "I thought you wanted to see Estabo get what he has coming to him. I guess I was wrong." Shrugging, he made as if to leave.

"Hold on there!" Telfar said. He gnawed on his lower lip a bit, then frowned, folded the switchblade and slid the knife into his pocket. "All right, Fed. You win. But it's a fine kettle of fish when an upstanding taxpayer like myself isn't entitled to a few measly dollars for selling out one of his own."

"I'm listening."

The sailor leaned against the brick wall. "It all started about two years ago. That's when a bigwig in Colombia bought the *Cartagena*, fired the old captain, who was a good buddy of mine, and hired Estabo. Everyone knows that he's as slimy as the day is long. So it didn't surprise me none when I heard tell that he was involved in drugs."

Bolan was disappointed. He needed hard facts, not barroom gossip.

"I knew the talk must be true when the *Cartagena*

disappeared for a whole month. Then there was that dirty business with the boy from Argentina—''

"Wait a second," Bolan interrupted. "How can a ship that size disappear? What do you mean?"

Telfar opened his mouth to reply. He suddenly stiffened, and his eyes went wide. "Look out!" he cried. "Behind you!"

Bolan started to turn, but the warning came too late. Two or three burly forms rammed into him from behind, and the next moment he was smashed to the asphalt.

5

Outweighed and outnumbered, the Executioner absorbed a hail of blows on his shoulders and back. One of his attackers roughly flipped him over. A fist was poised to smash into his jaw.

Bolan exploded, spiking a heel into the groin of the sailor about to punch him, then sweeping his legs against those of another husky adversary, who sprawled flat. One more assailant loomed above the soldier, a gangly seafarer who jerked a blackjack from a pocket and raised it to strike.

Throwing himself to one side, Bolan rose as the blackjack whizzed past his ear. A snap kick to the shin brought the gangly man's chin within reach, and an uppercut jolted him back.

For a few seconds Bolan was in the clear. Out of the corner of an eye he saw Telfar battling two others. Before he could turn to lend a hand, the three who had jumped him had regrouped and were closing in again. Grim, silent, they spread out, the man with the blackjack hefting it eagerly.

Someone else appeared at the mouth of the alley. It was Captain Estabo, wearing a sadistic smirk, his hands in his pockets. "Don't take all night," he snapped.

Bolan didn't go for the Beretta. None of the sailors was trying to kill him, only attempting to knock him out. If they wanted him dead, they would have pulled knives or guns. He figured that the captain merely meant to teach Telfar a lesson by having the man beaten senseless.

Telfar had gone down swinging. The three confronting Bolan glanced at one another, then charged. The soldier slipped a jab, countered with a right hook. The blackjack whistled toward his temple, but he blocked it with a forearm and returned the favor by boxing the sailor's ear. Yelping, the man drew back.

The third seaman was cannier. While Bolan focused on his friends, he slipped in around the Executioner and sprang. The first inkling Bolan had that the man was behind him came when a stout arm looped around his throat and whipped him backward so savagely that he thought his neck would break. His windpipe was choked off before he could take a deep breath.

"Got you, matey!" the man crowed.

A simple judo toss showed the braggart how wrong he was. Bolan gripped the sailor's arm, tucked at the waist and sent the man flying over his shoulder.

As Bolan straightened, Blackjack came at him again, aiming at the crown of his head. The soldier sidestepped, grabbed the man's wrist as it descended and levered him into a somersault that ended with the seaman thudding into the brick wall and falling flat, dazed.

The other two moved warily toward him. They had tasted the power in his fists and weren't hungry for a second helping. Bolan backed against the wall. He tensed to take the fight to them, but froze at a raspy command.

"That'll be enough out of you, Fed, or this worthless piece of trash meets his Maker."

Estabo no longer stood at the alley mouth. He had one knee pressed on top of Telfar's chest. The groggy sailor tried to rise but was held fast by the two crewmen from the *Cartagena*. The captain held the tip of a dagger pressed to Telfar's throat. A strand of blood crept across the flesh.

Bolan raised his hands to his shoulders. Even though it was tempting to go for the Beretta, he knew that Estabo could slice Telfar's jugular before he drew. And never, ever, would Bolan endanger an innocent life.

"That's better," the captain said, then nodded at the two men near Bolan.

A knife was jabbed against the soldier's ribs. He had to stand meekly and submit to a body search that yielded the Beretta plus a throwing knife strapped to his ankle. To add insult to injury, his own Beretta was then used to cover him.

Blackjack groaned. One of the men moved to help him as the pair holding Telfar straightened and stepped back.

Estabo, though, didn't rise. He slapped Telfar on the cheek, saying, "Snap out of it, scumbag. I want you to be awake. I want you to feel it."

"No!" Bolan said, almost lunging.

The Beretta fixed on a point between his eyes.

"Stay out of this, Fed," Estabo said flatly. "This is between my old friend and me." He gave Telfar another slap.

The grizzled sailor blinked a few times. Comprehension dawned, and he hissed, "Get off me, you lowlife! I won't be manhandled by the likes of you!"

The expression that came over the captain was a vivid portrait of evil incarnate. "I don't soil my hands on garbage."

"Big talk from a coward who had his crew jump me instead of going at it man to man!" Telfar took no heed of the dagger pressed against his throat. He spit full in Estabo's face. "There! Maybe that will clean off some of the slime!"

"You always were an idiot," Estabo said, and slit Telfar from ear to ear. It happened too fast for the eye to follow.

Telfar flinched, as if he had only been pricked. He didn't seem to realize how gravely he had been cut until he went to speak and blood spurted from his mouth. Sputtering, he clutched at his neck and stared in horror at his drenched hands.

Estabo had taken a short step to the right. "Any last words, stool pigeon?"

Whatever Telfar wanted to say came out as blubbered bubbles of blood. He rolled onto his side and attempted to stand. His arms shook, and his body quivered. He collapsed, helpless. The whites of his eyes showing, he looked desperately about him, as if for salvation that wasn't there. A ruby puddle formed under him, growing rapidly by the second.

Estabo showed no emotion as Telfar broke into violent convulsions that lasted less than a minute. When the body stilled, the captain squatted and wiped his dagger clean on Telfar's pants. Then he slipped the weapon under his pea jacket.

"That's exactly what will happen to you if you give me any trouble on the way to the ship," he said to Bolan.

At a gesture from Estabo, Bolan was ringed by sailors. His own Beretta was jammed into the base of his back, while on either side seamen draped arms over his shoulders and held knives close to his chest.

Estabo led them from the alley. Once on the street, several of the sailors commenced singing. They deliberately slurred words to make it appear as if they were a typical bunch of rowdy seamen returning from a lively evening in town. The strategy worked. No one gave them a second glance until they were at the waterfront and approaching the *Cartagena*. That was when a bearded man smoking a pipe slowed to have words with Estabo, asking when the coastal freighter was set to sail and when she would be returning from her run to South America. Estabo never once betrayed any nervousness. The man was an iceberg inside.

Bolan was ushered up the gangway to the foredeck. Other sailors converged and were addressed by their captain in Spanish. Bolan caught snatches here and there, enough to know that Estabo had kept him alive to learn how much the Feds knew about the drug ring's operation.

Given that Estabo was so open with his men, Bo-

Ian realized that most of the crew, if not all, were part of the ring. He was hustled below, down a narrow companionway to a small room. A swarthy sailor pushed him inside and slammed the door. A key rasped in the lock.

As soon as the seamen were gone, Bolan prowled his prison, seeking a means of escape. It was hopeless. The bulkheads, naturally, were solid metal. Nothing short of a bazooka would rupture them. And other than the locked door and a small porthole, there was no way in or out.

A bed, a table and chair were the only furniture. Bolan sat on the edge of the bed and pondered the situation. It was doubtful Estabo would murder him in port. The smuggler would wait until the ship was on the open sea to do with Bolan as he wanted, without any risk of interference. He had until then to come up with a brainstorm.

An hour went by. Bolan stretched out on the bed with his head propped in his hands. He was due to contact Brognola in another two hours. If the big Fed didn't hear from him, a strike team would be sent in. But they had no clue as to his fate. They could hunt until doomsday and never find him.

The key rattled again. The door was shoved inward so that it banged against the wall. In strode Estabo flanked by two crewmen with pistols, one holding Bolan's Beretta.

The captain swung the chair around and straddled it. "I would like to know your name," he said pleasantly enough.

"Pick any one you like." Bolan wasn't going to

give an inch, no matter how friendly Estabo acted. It was a sham. Sooner or later Estabo intended to kill him.

"Very well. How about if I call you Fed?" Estabo grinned without warmth and folded his hands over a knee. "I don't have much time to spare right now. Later, once we're under way, I will. Then you will tell me everything I need to know, whether you want to or not."

"Don't count on it," Bolan said.

Estabo acted as if he didn't hear. "What agency are you with? How did they find out about us? What have they uncovered so far?"

Recalling Telfar's revelations, the soldier tried a bluff. "We know all about the new owner of the *Cartagena,* about the time the ship vanished for a whole month and the truth about the boy from Argentina."

One of the gunners gasped.

The captain didn't so much as twitch a muscle for the longest while. Bolan began to think his ruse had been a bust. Then Estabo spoke, an edge to his voice. "I see. Then you know much more than I expected. El Gato will be most displeased. The only way you could have learned about his involvement and the retrofitting and Espinosa's murder is through an informer. El Gato will weed out whoever it is and skin him alive before feeding the turncoat to the barracudas."

In one fell swoop, Bolan had learned the nickname of the mastermind behind the whole drug ring, verified the fact that the freighter had undergone a major refitting and confirmed that the Argentine youth had indeed met with foul play. He wanted to fish for more information, but caution was called for. A single slip of the tongue would spoil everything. "It was the murder that led us to you."

"Was it?" Estabo sighed. "I had hoped no one would notice those slight marks on his wrists. We used strips from a towel to bind him before he was hung from the stern." His features hardened. "The young fool! I was told that he was dependable. But as soon as he learned the truth about us, he made the mistake of saying he would go to the authorities at our next port of call."

Bolan now knew that every last member of the crew was part of the operation. He was up against twenty or more hardened thugs. Not exactly the best of odds.

"Well, we will not make the same mistake with you. Once we reclaim the sub, we will weight you down with cinder blocks and dump you over the side. That should put an end to government snooping for a while."

"Killing me won't solve your problem," Bolan said. "Before long we'll have El Gato in custody."

The smuggler pursed his lips. "I think not. Even if your government knew where to find the sub pens, taking him into custody will not be easy. The place is a fortress. And the Colombian government is not about to let the United States military invade its soil."

Bolan was acquiring useful intel by the second. The only problem would be in relaying it to Brognola. "You'd be surprised. Where there's a will, there's a way."

Estabo stood, his brow knit. "You have given me much to think about, Fed. We will talk again. Until then, try nothing stupid. For your own sake."

The door clanged shut. Bolan was left alone with his thoughts. Gradually the full scope of the drug-smuggling operation dawned on him.

Whoever El Gato, or "the Cat," happened to be, the man threatened to flood the world with more coke than had ever been available at any one time in all of human history.

The Cat already had at least two minisubmarines at his disposal. Based on what little Bolan knew of subs that size, he guessed that each was able to carry up to two tons of cocaine at a time.

Since the *Cartagena* made two trips to the U.S. every thirty days, the sub had to be funneling four tons of the white powder in a month. Multiply that by two to take into account the sub operating along the California coast, and it meant that eight tons of snow hit the streets of America as regular as clockwork.

Unless the Cat was stopped, it promised to get even worse. The mention of sub pens indicated to Bolan that more submersibles were going to be put into service, if they hadn't been already. For all he knew, the Cat's grand scheme called for a fleet of minisubs.

There would be no holding back the flood of co-caine. Governments around the globe would be helpless to stem the tide. The toll taken on America alone would be devastating.

Bolan made a mental vow right then and there that come what may, he was going to take the Cat down. Somehow he would get off the ship and get word to Brognola.

The night went by without incident. Bolan was left alone until shortly after sunrise when a tray of food was brought by a man in a white apron. Two sailors made sure Bolan didn't try anything while the tray was placed on the table.

Not one to look a gift horse in the mouth, the soldier ate heartily. Common sense told him that he had to keep his strength up for later on.

Shortly after the cook had returned to take the tray away, the door opened once more, and in walked Estabo. A pair of seamen was told to wait outside.

"Good morning, Fed," the captain said cheerily. "I trust you enjoyed your meal."

"A last treat for the condemned man?" Bolan said.

"Nothing quite so barbaric. It will be four or five days yet until we get around to dumping you in the ocean, and I see no reason to starve you until then."

Was that the real reason? Bolan wondered. Or did Estabo want him to grow accustomed to the meals so that they could slip something into his food on the big day to render him helpless to resist? A few knockout drops in his coffee would do the trick nicely. He'd be breathing water before he knew what hit him.

"We get under way in about twenty minutes," Estabo said.

Normally the soldier wouldn't say two words to his captor. But psychological manipulation could work two ways. Estabo wanted him to be as tame as a kitten. Conversely he wanted the smuggler to think that he would rather talk his way out of his fix than try to escape. "I don't suppose you'd care to save us both a lot of trouble and turn yourself in before we do?"

Estabo laughed. "You amuse me, American. I hope you will prove equally entertaining when it comes time to question you." He turned to go.

"Maybe you could strike a deal with the government," Bolan remarked.

That brought the captain up short. He glanced at the doorway, lowered his voice and said, "What kind of deal?"

Bolan shrugged. "I'm not the one you need to talk to. But they might be willing to grant some form of immunity from prosecution in exchange for your testimony against the Cat."

"Cross El Gato?" Estabo shook his head. "The last man who did that had his tongue cut out and his fingers chopped off before they got around to prying his eyeballs from his face. Not to mention what the barracudas did to him. No thanks, Fed. I am too fond of breathing."

The door clanged shut. Bolan listened. On the deck above, a swirl of activity was taking place as the crew prepared to depart. Orders were barked; the anchor chain clanked. For a while the smugglers would be too busy to give any thought to him.

Sliding onto the floor, Bolan lay on his back to examine the underside of the bed. Several times during the night it had creaked when he changed position. Sure enough, a small box spring supported the mattress.

All the comforts of home, Bolan mused as he applied his fingers to one of the coils. The wire was thick, next to impossible to bend. Wriggling underneath, he probed the edges of the box spring. Near the middle, where the springs had to bear the greatest weight, a connecting wire between a pair of coils had been nearly snapped in two. After considerable twisting and prying, Bolan managed to break it completely, then began to unravel as long a piece as he could.

It was like trying to unwind high-tensile steel, a slow, tedious, painstaking process. But he persevered, all of that day and half the next, stopping whenever footsteps thumped in the passageway.

No midday or evening meals were brought to him. Breakfast was served by the same cook. Estabo didn't put in an appearance until the middle of the afternoon, and by then Bolan had a two-foot coil of wire hidden under the mattress.

The captain's expression was troubled. He gave the soldier a probing stare as he took his seat. "I thought you were lying, you know," he began.

"About what?" Bolan said.

"Everything. There was no way your government could have linked Espinosa's death to our network.

At the worst, they would have chalked it up to a common murder. Nothing more.''

Bolan made no comment. He waited to see what was on the other man's mind.

"But now I am not so sure," Estabo said. "I have learned that one of our local operations has been put out of business—"

The Executioner put two and two together. "Key West."

Estabo appeared startled. "You know about it? Then things are worse than I imagined."

"It's never too late to strike a deal." Bolan didn't really expect the captain to take him up on the offer. It was a ploy to give Estabo second thoughts about snuffing him. Any delay worked in his favor.

The captain rose and paced in front of the door, hands clasped behind his back. "Maybe as a last resort," he said, more to himself than to Bolan. "But until that time comes, I must take whatever steps are necessary to protect myself and all those who work under me."

Bolan was perched on the edge of the bunk. He contemplated grabbing the wire and using it on Estabo if the captain turned his back, but discarded the idea. The guards outside would gun him down before he got ten feet.

The smuggler nodded at the porthole. "In case you haven't noticed, we are only moving at five to seven knots so we will still be within range of the Keys when night falls." He stopped pacing. "The sub must spend the rest of the day recharging its batteries so it can rendezvous with us after dark." Estabo added, almost as an afterthought, "Thankfully it is a sunny day."

There was only one reason that would be important. "The minisubs are solar powered?" Bolan asked in surprise.

Estabo smirked. "At last something you do not know. Yes, Fed. El Gato spent a fortune to fit the subs with retractable solar panels. The energy is stored in a bank of special batteries. I'm no expert, but I understand no one has ever developed a system like the one they use."

Bolan was impressed. It was another stroke of genius on the Cat's part. Relying on solar power spared the subs the necessity of having to refuel regularly, which would add to the risk of detection.

At that moment a low drone sounded overhead. Bolan recognized it as the growl of a plane engine.

Estabo also noticed. "Friends of yours, I take it? Three times today a seaplane has flown low over us." He rapped on the door and a sailor outside opened it. "They are wasting their time, though. By morning you will be at the bottom of the sea."

This time the clang of the door was like the final note of a death dirge. Bolan waited until the footsteps faded, then he took out the wire and unrolled it. At each end he fashioned loops just big enough to slip his fingers through. Sliding one of the loops under his sleeve, he pushed the wire up his arm until the loop nestled snugly under his armpit.

He was as ready as he would ever be. All he had to do was move his arm a fraction outward and the wire would slip down into his palm.

Time dragged; the afternoon waned. When the light out the porthole began to fade, the *Cartagena* slowed to a virtual crawl. A minute later Bolan heard someone approach. The key was inserted into the lock.

There were two of them, as usual, the same pair who had accompanied Estabo the first time. One held the soldier's Beretta. "On your feet, mister," he snapped. "It's time to pay the piper."

6

The Executioner was marched aft. One sailor walked in front of him, the other behind. A maze of passageways had to be negotiated. Bolan tried to keep track of the route they took, but it was a hopeless cause.

Now and then they passed other crew members. Most gave Bolan the sort of look they might give a venomous snake they wanted to stomp on.

Deep in the bowels of the vessel, they came to a companionway. They descended, their footsteps pinging hollowly.

No one else was on the steps. Lights were few and far between, so shadows were everywhere. Bolan would never have a better opportunity.

He made his move as they neared another landing. The man in front was peering over the rail toward the bottom. A quick glance showed that the seaman with the Beretta was scratching his chin and yawning. They didn't know enough to keep their eyes on their prisoner every second. But then, they were smugglers, not hit men.

Bolan burst into motion. His right foot lashed forward, catching the sailor two steps below him in the kidney and knocking him into the rail. At the same time he spun, and his left fist swatted the Beretta's muzzle away from his head.

The kicked crewman nearly pitched over the side. He had to drop his pistol and clutch at the rail with both hands as his body tilted forward, his legs flapping the air. Struggling mightily, he tried to pull himself back up.

In the same span of time, the soldier had slipped in behind the sailor with the Beretta, evading a hastily thrown left cross. As Bolan moved, he relaxed the pressure of his arm on the makeshift garrote. The loop at the bottom fell smoothly into his hand. In a flash he had the garrote out.

As the sailor began to turn, Bolan slipped the wire over the man's head, crossed the ends and tightened.

The man choked, gasping for air as the wire bit into his skin. He clawed at the garrote, his fingernails unable to gain a grip. Wheezing and thrashing, he pointed the Beretta behind him.

Bolan kneed the smuggler in the back, driving the crewman against the side rail while clamping on the wire with all his might. His muscles bulged. The garrote dug in farther, driving the sailor into a frenzy.

The Beretta clattered onto the step at their feet.

Meanwhile the other seaman had almost made it back over the rail. He hooked a foot to gain purchase and fell onto his side close to his gun. "You're dead meat!" he huffed, and scrambled toward it.

The garrote had served its purpose. Bolan scooped up the Beretta on the fly as he sprang onto the lower step next to the scrambling seaman. The man's hand closed on the pistol, and he began to rise.

Bolan jammed the Beretta against the sailor's ribs to muffle the report and stroked the trigger twice. Parabellum manglers chewed up the man's insides, one exiting under the bottom rib and ricocheting off the steps. The seaman dropped into a heap, exhaling his last breath as blood seeped from the corners of his mouth.

Crouching, Bolan cocked an ear and heard nothing other than the throb of the freighter's engines. He slid the Beretta into his shoulder rig, wedged the other pistol, a 9 mm Taurus, under his belt and hastily dragged the bodies to the next landing, aligning them against the wall in murky shadow. If things went well, no one would notice them until he was off the vessel.

How to accomplish that was the big question. His best bet was to go topside, find a rope, then climb down over the hull before someone spotted him and the crew converged like a pack of rabid wolves.

Any spare rope was likely to be stored at the stern, where the superstructure was located.

Bolan left the companionway and headed aft. He came to a junction. Faint footsteps sounded off to the left, so he went to the right. He had gone only a dozen feet when the *Cartagena*'s engines were throttled back. Farther aft, a loud grating sound echoed through the ship. It resembled the grinding of gears, or the noise a rusty door being pried open might make. He also heard yells.

Estabo had let it slip to him that the freighter would rendezvous with the minisub after the sun went down. The noises had to be connected to the sub's arrival.

At the next junction, Bolan turned to the left, toward the sounds. He had to see for himself how it was done. The odds of discovery were high, but the risk was acceptable if it helped Brognola put an end to the smuggling ring.

So far no crewmen had appeared. Bolan reasoned that those not on duty above deck were busy helping with the sub. He came to a door already open a crack and pushed on it. Instantly he realized his mistake and flattened against the bulkhead.

He had come upon an enormous hold that was crammed with cargo. Several crew members were busy shuttling crates around on a forklift.

Keeping his eyes on them, Bolan eased onto a catwalk that led toward the port side of the vessel. At the end was another door leading into a passageway that ran aft. It, in turn, brought him to a smaller hold only half-filled. As he scanned the pallets, a sailor came through a door at the bottom of the hold on the starboard side.

Squatting, Bolan observed the sailor cross to the forward bulkhead and scale metal rungs to another catwalk. The man then vanished down a passageway.

The Executioner studied the door at the bottom. It was camouflaged so well that if he hadn't seen the seaman come out, he would never have known it was there. He had to see what was on the other side.

There were more rungs. He went down rapidly. Ducking in between the cargo, he stealthily neared the door. A slender latch had been cleverly concealed as a joint in the wall. It clicked at his tug, but quietly. Cracking the door, he pressed an eye to the slit.

El Gato didn't miss a trick.

The retrofit Estabo had told Bolan about had involved much more than installing the latest hardware. A new bulkhead had been erected across one end of the hold to divide it into two sections. The larger section was the hold itself. The smaller section became a hidden compartment for the minisub.

Since there had to be a way for the submersible to get on and off the ship, a one-hundred-foot portion of the starboard hull could be lowered and raised at will, thanks to a heavy winch. Once the hull section was lowered, the sub was lifted by a recessed gantry and swiveled into its berth in the compartment.

Bolan had never seen anything quite like it. The whole operation was as slick as a whistle.

No doubt the cocaine was loaded in Colombia, then the freighter would steam north to the Gulf of Mexico until it reached a designated point west of the Keys. There the *Cartagena* would briefly stop so the sub could be lowered. Then the ship would go on its way with no one the wiser.

It was a perfect setup. While the freighter unloaded its legal cargo in a port of call, the minisub unloaded its illegal cargo on Dominique Island. Until a few nights ago, it had been José Santoro's job to pick up the coke and funnel it to the mainland.

A similar setup was probably in operation on the West Coast. Once the Feds found out, they might be able to track down the freighter involved.

At that moment the minisub floated in the water

beside the hull. Six crewmen were busy attaching it to the gigantic sling that hung from the gantry. Four more sailors were engaged in various tasks. Overseeing it all was Captain Estabo, who stood just a few yards away with his back to the soldier. Floodlights illuminated the entire scene.

Bolan started to shut the door. While the captain was occupied, the Executioner would sneak onto the upper deck and find the rope he needed.

At that split second a gruff voice bellowed almost in his ear. "Hey! Who are you? What are you doing here?"

It was the sailor who had left a few minutes earlier. He had returned bearing a large crescent wrench. As Bolan whirled, the seaman raised the wrench to strike a blow. The Executioner flicked a jab that rocked the man on his heels. A solid right keeled him over.

But the harm has been done. Shouts rang out, and the door was flung wide, framing Estabo, who took one look at Bolan and roared, "Over here! It's the Fed!" He reached under his pea jacket and flourished the switchblade.

Bolan didn't bother to run for it. For one thing he would be a sitting duck as he climbed the rungs. For another, it would only be a matter of time before the crew hunted him down once Estabo alerted them.

The Executioner went on the offensive, charging the doorway as the captain angled the switchblade to slash. Estabo didn't appear to notice that Bolan had drawn the Beretta. The 9 mm pistol cracked once. A red-rimmed hole blossomed in the center of the captain's forehead, and he staggered into a couple of seamen rushing to help him.

Bolan ran into the sub compartment. All work had stopped. A few of the sailors were frozen in shock, but the rest were either hurrying toward him, unlimbering guns, or drawing blades.

The soldier pulled the Taurus on the fly. With a pistol in each hand he sprinted toward the section of the hull that had opened. A man came at him with a dirk, and Bolan shot him through the chest. Another sailor stood on top of the sub, taking aim with a revolver. A round from the Taurus flipped him into the sea.

Then Bolan was at the rim of the open hull. Before him stretched the vast expanse of the gulf. A shot split the air as he dived, his arms over his head so that he slashed into the water cleanly. Down he went, as deep as he could go, kicking and pumping, while all the time lead zipped through the water on either side and in front and back.

Swimming toward the stern, Bolan glimpsed the ship's large propellers off to his right. He was nearly abreast of them when he had to go up for air. The moment his head broke the surface, the floodlight caught him in its glare and gunfire erupted from the sub compartment. Pistols and revolvers boomed a symphony.

Bolan kept going. Once he was around the stern, they wouldn't be able to see him. He stroked smoothly, the pistols still in his hands. Pausing to shove them under his belt, he suddenly became aware of a new threat as spotlights washed over him from overhead. Autofire peppered the water, coming from a gunner on the quarter deck. Bolan could see the man's head and shoulders, but little else. He resumed swimming, faster than ever.

The hail of lead only stopped when the gunner's magazine emptied. In seconds he had slapped in a new one. By then Bolan was close to the stern.

The *Cartagena*'s hull reared above him. The shots tapered off. Bolan was astern of the vessel, making for the port side. He didn't dwell on the fact that the reprieve was only temporary. More gunners would man the upper decks.

Bolan stayed close to the hull, where the slant of the ship hid him from the enemy guns. Treading water, he gazed eastward, hoping to spot an island in the distance. But he should have known the rendezvous site would be far from the Keys and possible prying eyes. They were in the middle of the gulf.

A racket on the starboard side told Bolan the minisub was being hoisted into the ship. Soon the freighter would get under way. Maybe, he reflected, they intended to come about and run him down. He had to put distance between himself and the vessel.

Bolan swam eastward, his skin prickling in anticipation of the first volley. Spotlights pegged him squarely. Four or five guns cut loose simultaneously. Slugs hissed into the water so close to him that tiny geysers sprayed his face.

He dived again, going deep, then traveling as far as he could before his lungs screamed for air. Rising, he quickly filled them, then dived again. Each time he surfaced, a volley of shots drilled into the water around him. But he was never up long enough for any of the rounds to score.

Bolan heard a strange rasping noise from high on the *Cartagena*. Since no shots greeted his appearance, he rotated.

A lifeboat was being lowered. Filled with armed sailors, it was being winched down a few feet at a time.

Bolan swam for his life. Some of the sailors on deck broke into whoops and hollers, taunting him, having fun at his expense.

Fatigue nipped at Bolan's limbs, but he refused to give in to it. Settling into a steady rhythm, he stroked smoothly. Twice he glanced back. The last time, the lifeboat was in the water and turning in his direction. A spotlight mounted on the bow appeared toward him. Oars rose and fell.

Cheers erupted on the *Cartagena* as the lifeboat gained. Two sailors armed with rifles stepped to the bow. The leaner of the pair pressed a stock to his shoulder.

Bolan veered to the left. A slug smacked into the water inches from his shoulder even as the shot rumbled off across the gulf. He slanted to the right, the left and the right again. A second shot missed.

Laughter and hoots spurred the riflemen to try harder.

Plowing ahead, Bolan heard a high-powered round churn the water at his elbow. Trying to outrun them was useless. Suddenly stopping, he drew the Beretta. Choppy waves made fixing a bead difficult, but he elevated the barrel and snapped off a shot anyway.

He was rewarded by the sight of the lean shooter stumbling backward.

The return fire angered the seamen. Their oars rose and fell with renewed vigor. The lifeboat was now within sixty feet and closing fast. Bolan saw the other rifleman take precise aim.

At that moment, with the Executioner's life hanging in the balance, a seaplane roared in low over the freighter, coming from the west. The near wing dipped and an M-60 opened up. Shrieking rounds ate into the lifeboat and its occupants like a horde of termites into wood. The rifleman was the first to topple, his torso riddled with walnut-sized holes. Four more hardmen were taken out of the play, then the lifeboat splintered, its punctured hull unable to sustain the weight of its occupants.

The unmarked black amphibian banked tightly, sweeping low and making a smooth landing. Twin props chugging, it shot straight toward Bolan. The cockpit windscreen and the gun blisters were tinted, so he couldn't see who was at the controls.

Roars of outrage rose in a chorus from the deck of the freighter. Hot lead spewed at the incoming aircraft, but most of the slugs fell short. A few pinged off the wings and fuselage, doing no real damage.

Bolan swam to meet the big bird, which had slowed to a coasting crawl and swung broadside. A door opened and a rope ladder unfurled, smacking the water. The soldier reached it and climbed. Muffled voices sounded above him. One, louder than the rest, said, "Move over. I want to have the honors."

It was a voice the Executioner recognized. Almost

to the top, he glanced up into the grinning face of Jack Grimaldi, Stony Man Farm's ace pilot and one of Mack Bolan's friends.

"Good to see you, Sarge. Thought I'd drop by to pull your fat out of the fire."

SIX HOURS LATER, after a shower, a meal and some rest, the Executioner was in another aircraft, this time a General Dynamics F-111F. A pair of Pratt & Whitney TF30-PW-100 turbofan engines propelled the Air Force fighter westward at a speed of Mach 2 at its service ceiling of 60,000 feet.

Jack Grimaldi sat at the controls, whistling softly to himself. The ace pilot loved flying, loved excitement, loved his country. His job enabled him to fulfill all three passions, so it was little wonder he was invariably in a good mood.

They were en route to California. Bolan had put in a call to Hal Brognola and filled the big Fed in the moment he arrived on the mainland. Shortly before leaving for California, the Justice man had gotten back to him. His team was in the process of running a computer check of freighters that routinely docked in the San Francisco area. It was a daunting challenge, as the harbor was one of the busiest in the world.

"It'll take a while to pin down the likeliest vessel," Brognola had told Bolan. "By the time you arrive on the coast, I should have something for you."

Brognola had better luck with the mastermind of

the operation, El Gato. He was already on file, although the file was inactive. It seemed El Gato was supposed to be dead.

His real name was Estavan Quesada. He had been born in Bogotá. His mother had been a prostitute, his father her pimp. At the tender age of twelve he had been left an orphan when a john stabbed his mother to death and his father had been mortally wounded going to her aid.

Quesada had gone to live with an uncle, but there was some sort of incident, and six months later he was a street urchin, living by his wits and his fists, stealing to get by.

By the age of sixteen, Quesada was the leader of a gang of toughs who terrorized a poorer section of Bogotá. He earned a reputation as an expert with a knife, as well as the nickname El Gato for his speed and savagery.

Quesada was arrested twice, once for robbery, once for assault. Each time, he was let off with a slap on the wrist.

Somewhere along the line, he delved into the drug trade and became a dealer. Perhaps due to his age, he was adept at luring kids into the gloomy underworld of drug addiction. He so impressed his boss, Fernando Chavez, that he moved up through the ranks quickly to become one of Chavez's trusted lieutenants.

But that wasn't good enough for Quesada.

In one fell swoop he butchered his patron and three other lieutenants.

Colombian authorities were keeping tabs on him,

but try as they might, they were unable to gather a shred of solid evidence against him. Informants mysteriously disappeared. So did a highly respected detective who had been close to bringing Quesada down.

At the same time, Quesada continued to move up in the world. It wasn't long before he controlled all of Bogotá. Drugs, stolen goods, smuggled arms, the prostitution trade, they were all under his thumb. He went into partnership with the Medellín cartel. The money poured in. He had bank accounts in Switzerland, a retreat in the Bahamas, a ranch in Mexico. He had it all. And then his world came crashing down.

Ironically one of Quesada's own lieutenants turned on him after El Gato trifled with his wife. Colombian police obtained a warrant for Quesada's arrest and surrounded his estate. A bloody battle claimed the lives of nine officers and fourteen of the drug lord's soldiers. Somehow the main house was set ablaze. In the rubble the police found Quesada's remains. Or so a pathologist claimed.

"Obviously the pathologist was bought off," Brognola had commented over the phone. "Quesada wised up and went underground. Now he's back in a big way."

Which was the understatement of the century. If it was true that money was power, then El Gato might well become one of the most powerful men in history.

Mack Bolan wasn't going to let that happen. He would put Quesada out of business permanently, no matter what it took.

7

"We have her on radar, sir."

Captain Jayce Gowen nodded. "Steady as she goes, helmsman. I don't want them to know we're here until they launch the sub."

"Aye, sir."

The Executioner stood on the bridge of the Coast Guard cutter *Liberty,* the pockets of his blacksuit crammed with the tools of his lethal trade. As far as the Coast Guard personnel knew, he was Commander Mike Belasko, on special assignment. He saw unasked questions in the eyes of Gowen every time he looked at the man, but the rugged officer had the decency not to pry.

Brognola's people had traced a vessel with a possible link to El Gato. It was a refrigerator ship called the *Parismina,* and it made regular runs from South America to the West Coast. Although it flew an Argentine flag and often brought Argentine beef to the U.S., it was owned by the same Colombia company that owned the *Cartagena.*

Which wasn't unusual. A vessel owned by a firm in one country might be registered in a different country because the second country levied fewer or no taxes on ships, allowed the owners to pay lower wages or required fewer costly safety measures. As always it was the bottom line that mattered most. Many shipping companies would do whatever it took to hike their profit margins.

Discreet checking had uncovered that the *Parismina* was on her way north and would soon dock in San Francisco. Through proper channels Brognola had seen to it that a Coast Guard cutter was dispatched, and that Bolan was on board.

Gowen glanced at Bolan. "Since you're supposed to be the expert here, mind telling me what type of armament we'll be up against?"

"Small arms, rifles and SMGs mostly. And the torpedoes on the sub."

The officer's jaw muscles twitched. "Just between you and me, Commander, I can't wait to pay them back for what they did to Lieutenant Bergan and his crew. I knew George well. He was a good man."

The *Parismina* was off Monterey Bay, steaming north. The *Liberty* shadowed her, hugging the coast. It was late afternoon, the emerald sea shimmering with a sheen of brilliant light.

Bolan stayed to one side, out of everyone's way. The grim crew rarely spoke except in the line of duty. They had heard about the patrol boat, and they wanted a piece of those responsible.

"Captain, the *Parismina* is slowing," the radar operator reported. "She's dropped from twenty-eight knots to twenty for no apparent reason."

"Let me know when she's dead in the water," Gowen said.

The soldier glanced westward, and remembered.

"If they follow the same pattern here that they did in the Gulf, they won't release the sub until after the sun sets."

"Wonderful," Gowen muttered.

"She's down to ten knots and still falling, sir," the radar operator revealed.

Gowen turned to the seaman at the helm. "Match her knot for knot."

"Yes, sir."

"Five knots now, and holding steady."

Bolan nodded. "Just like in the gulf."

The *Liberty*'s commanding officer motioned and led the way onto the deck. Leaning on the rail, Gowen said, "Listen, Commander. Far be it for me to pry. I was told not to ask questions, and I always follow orders. But it's obvious you've had dealings with these people before." He gestured at several seamen manning a five-inch gun. "The lives of all my men are at stake here. It would help me immensely if I knew as much as you do."

The man had a valid point. Bolan had no objections to sharing the bare-bones details of his clash with the crew of the *Cartagena*. He finished with, "It won't be a cakewalk. These smugglers are as vicious as they come. Odds are they won't surrender without a fight."

"I wouldn't have it any other way," Gowen replied. He stared thoughtfully at the sea. "Based on what you've just told me, our best bet is to catch them with their pants down." He rapped on the rail a few times, excited by his train of thought. "We need to attack after they open the sub compartment but before they swing the gantry into position to release the sub. That way they won't be able to go anywhere without flooding their hull. And the sub will be stranded high and dry, so to speak.''

It was excellent strategy, and Bolan said so.

"On which side of the freighter was the sub compartment located?''

"Starboard.''

Gowen chuckled and rubbed his hands together. "If they did the same with the *Parismina*, we have them dead to rights. Her starboard side is facing us.''

Hours passed. Since there was no way of knowing if the refrigerator ship carried sophisticated monitoring equipment, the cutter maintained radio silence.

At length the sun rested on the rim of the world. The ocean was dappled with streaks of red and orange. The *Parismina* steered northwesterly until she was two miles out, at which point she slowed to a crawl.

The *Liberty* stayed with her every foot of the way, never close enough to be seen, never letting her get out of radar range, either. The crew was subdued, just as men going into battle always were.

The captain was friendlier toward Bolan after they had their talk. He brought the soldier a cup of coffee, and later mentioned that if he was hungry, he was free to help himself in the galley. But the last thing on Bolan's mind was food.

Finally the sun sank. Another forty minutes elapsed before the radar operator had something new to pass along. "Captain! The *Parismina* has stopped!''

"You're certain?" Gowen responded.

"I'd stake my life on it. Her screw signatures are nil."

"Then this is the moment we've been waiting for!" Eagerly Gowen barked out orders. "Helmsman, hard to port! Full speed ahead! All hands, battle stations! I repeat! All hands to battle stations! Gunners, I want you locked on target the second she's in range!"

Bolan felt the deck shift ever so slightly under him as the orders were carried out. Like a great white shark moving in for the kill, the cutter bore down on her target at top speed.

Not having anything to do until they boarded, Bolan had to settle for the part of spectator. Watching the coastguardsmen perform was like watching the cogs of a well-oiled machine mesh in flawless action. They were every bit as competent as any Navy unit he had ever seen.

A petty officer brought a side arm for the captain, who strapped it tight around his waist and slapped the .45 pistol as if it were an old friend.

On the forecastle, a boarding detail of seamen armed with side arms and M-16s fell in. Nearby the sailors manning the five-inch gun had swiveled it toward their quarry and were loading a shell.

Suddenly the radar operator cried out, "Captain! They're trying to jam us!"

"They're what?" Gowen responded, and glanced sharply at Bolan, who shrugged. There had been no mention of electronic countersurveillance apparatus aboard the freighter in the gulf. "Well, let them! We're too close now for it to do them any good!"

Hardly were the words out of the officer's mouth than a tremendous geyser erupted off the port bow. The boom of the explosion was muted by the bulkheads.

"They're firing on us, sir!" a petty officer announced.

Gowen squared his shoulders. "I can see that for myself, Winslow," he said as calmly as if they were taking a luxury cruise instead of barreling headlong into the guns of an enemy vessel. "Fine. If that's the way they want to play it, then at my command, the gunnery crew will open fire." He paused for a five-count. *"Fire!"*

The cutter's gun thundered. In the distance the *Parismina* was now visible, her running lights aglow. Floodlights at her waterline marked where the mini-sub was being frantically hoisted from a secret compartment similar to the one on the *Cartagena*.

Bolan saw a flash of fire on the refrigerator ship's forecastle, another aft. Twin plumes of water on either side of the Coast Guard vessel confirmed there were two guns on the smuggler's ship.

The cutter never swerved. Gowen planted his feet and jutted his chin defiantly at the larger vessel. "Gunnery crew, fire at will!"

As the range decreased, the shells came closer and closer. It wasn't hard for Bolan to imagine how the *Parismina*'s guns had been disguised when not in use. The wily smugglers had probably built concealed compartments on the upper decks, just as they had belowdecks for the sub. Customs inspectors and other officials would never have caught on unless they went over the ship with a fine-tooth comb and measured every square inch to see if there were any discrepancies.

Suddenly a sheet of flame flared skyward amidships on the *Parismina*. A lusty cheer from the coastguardmen was silenced by their commanding officer.

"Belay that! There will be time enough for celebrating when we've boarded her and have every one of those pirates in custody! Not before!"

The *Liberty* rocked to a near miss. Spray splashed against the bridge, lending the illusion that the cutter was sinking.

Bolan saw another blast rip the *Parismina*'s superstructure. The Coast Guard gunners had the range and were making the most of it. Two more shells hit close by. Flames gusted, fanned by a stiff wind. Moments later the seamen scored a direct hit on the forward gun. A fireball arced into the air, illuminating the entire upper deck.

Lower down, in the glow of the floodlight, figures could be seen scampering about the sub, preparing it for launch. Already it had been hoisted from its compartment and swung out over the ocean. All that remained was for the smugglers to lower it. Then the refrigerator ship could raise the outer hull and get under way. It would have been simpler for the enemy to close the compartment with the sub still inside. If they had, they would already be steaming away.

There was a method to their madness, and Bolan

knew what it was. "They're trying to save the cocaine at all costs," he said.

Gowen looked at him, his eyes glinting. "Over my dead body."

He faced around. "Gunners! I want that sub blown sky high! Now!"

The gunnery crew lowered their big gun and fired. A watery plume drenched the sub and the smugglers, but the sub was spared.

"Again!"

The cutter unleashed a barrage of shells that struck the side of the refrigerator ship, struck the hidden compartment and struck the gantry. But not one hit the minisub. Bolan could hardly believe his eyes. It was as if the sub had a charmed existence. The last shell, though, blew the gantry to bits, and the submersible plummeted a good ten feet, smashing onto the surface with all the grace of a falling brick.

In the meantime the smugglers manning the aft gun nearly nailed the *Liberty*. A shell exploded dangerously near the port bow, ripping out a length of rail.

"Damn them!" Gowen growled. "Gunners! Take out that other gun!"

To Bolan, he said, "Sorry. First things first."

There was no need for the officer to apologize. Bolan would have done the same in Gowen's shoes. He looked up as fiery mushrooms sprouted near the stern of the *Parismina*. They danced their way forward, showering debris and ruptured body parts. Another instant, and the aft gun was silenced.

"Now the sub!" Gowen directed his gunners.

Bolan stepped forward for a better view. The mini-sub was in motion, seeking to get clear of the refrigerator ship before submerging. A geyser lifted its nose out of the water, but the sub stayed intact.

"Does the damn thing have nine lives?" Gowen snapped.

The next shell proved it didn't. The sub was slammed sideways. It rolled, then righted itself and slowly limped northward. Even without binoculars, Bolan could see that the rudder and propeller housing had been badly damaged. There was also a hole on the upper deck a few yards from the rudder.

Gowen shook a fist, elated. "Got her! She won't be able to submerge. We can finish her off at our leisure. Boarding party, get ready. Grappling hooks set. Lieutenant Hanover, you and your men be ready to provide covering fire."

Broken bodies and bits of debris floated near the shattered compartment. A section of outer hull had been twisted into so much scrap. Bolan studied the opening and had an idea. "Captain," he said, and pointed when Gowen turned. "Give me some men and we'll go in through there while you lead the boarding party over the top."

"Hit them high and low at the same time?" Gowen said. He clapped Bolan on the back. "I like the way you think, mister."

The captain faced a subordinate. "You heard the man, Ensign Palmer. Pick four men on the double. You're to go with Commander Belasko and kick major butt."

Palmer grinned like a kid given a gift he had always longed for, and saluted. "Aye, Captain. Four men coming right up."

Gowen leaned toward Bolan. "Watch out for him, will you? He has a good head on his shoulders, but this is his first action. Don't let the eager beaver get his head blown off."

"I'll try my best." Bolan trailed the officer from the bridge and down several steps to the deck. By then the Coast Guard cutter had slowed and was coming alongside the refrigerator ship. The enemy cut loose with automatic fire but not nearly as much as Bolan had expected. The coastguardsmen returned fire with fierce effect.

Thanks to the rent in the *Parismina*'s hull, the ship would take water and sink if the smugglers attempted to make a run for it. They had two options: surrender or fight. And they were clearly not disposed to giving up.

Scanning the rail high above, Bolan counted five hardmen firing down at the cutter. They were no more than inky silhouettes against the backdrop of spotlights, dappled now and again by roving searchlights on the Coast Guard vessel. He sighted on a man using what appeared to be an AK-47 assault rifle and triggered off three rounds from the M-16. The smuggler clutched at his head, whipped forward and hurtled over the rail to sink from sight between the two ships.

More coastguardsmen joined the fray, their combined firepower driving the smugglers back from the *Parismina*'s rail. Grappling hooks arched overhead. A few missed and fell back, but most snagged fast.

At the same time, Ensign Palmer and his four-man detail were lowering ropes over the sides of the cutter. Once the ropes were secure, he swung toward Bolan. "We're ready when you are, sir!"

Gowen gave the Executioner another clap on the back. "Godspeed, Commander! Give them hell!" Then, with a shout, flanked by dozens of seamen, he rushed toward the scaling ropes that would take the boarding party up onto the deck of the refrigerator ship.

Bolan raced to the side of the cutter. Without hesitation, he bent, grabbed a stout rope and swung down, bracing his feet against the hull. Like a mountain climber rappeling down a cliff, he dropped until he was eight feet above the ocean.

A few yards to Bolan's rear was the mangled section of the *Parismina*'s hull. Pushing off from the cutter, he swung precariously out over the twisted steel and let go. Spray from the shells had made the metal slick. Bolan slipped and nearly toppled into the water. Righting himself, he unslung the M-16 and hurried toward the ravaged sub compartment as Palmer and the seamen swooped toward the vessel.

Bolan paused at the jagged hole to cover the five men as they scurried over. A blast of cold air from the interior reminded the soldier that the ship was in reality a gigantic freezer, and that if the coolant lines had been ruptured, it would be as cold as an iceberg in there.

Palmer leaned against the other side of the opening and nodded. His youthful features shone with raw excitement.

"Stay behind me and do exactly as I say," Bolan whispered. Then, tucking the autorifle to his side, he entered the hold. A blanket of cold engulfed him, so frigid that he broke out in goose bumps and could see his breath in front of his face. Dim bulbs recessed in the ceiling revealed row upon row of sides of beef hanging from meat hooks.

Bolan stuck to an aisle between the rows. At double time he advanced toward the far end where a door was faintly visible. Outside, the firefight continued to rage, while feet pounded the deck above them. Men screamed and cursed. Explosions sounded aft.

The soldier was fifteen feet from the door when it unexpectedly opened. Three grimy smugglers armed with rifles and SMGs spilled into the hold.

Since Bolan already had the M-16 leveled, he merely needed to squeeze the trigger and sweep the barrel from right to left to take the enemy out of the play. Holes stitched the chest of each man. The trio died on their feet without getting off a shot.

Reaching the doorway, Bolan peered out at a narrow passageway. With a nod at the ensign, he darted into the open and sprinted toward a companionway. The coastguardsmen strung out in single file behind him.

The din of battle rose dramatically once they reached the steps. Somewhere a man screeched in anguish. Heavy-caliber weapons boomed, mixed with the metallic chatter of automatic hardware. Tendrils of smoke curled down from above, adding to a heavy acrid scent in the air. Flashes of light lent an eerie touch.

"Dear Lord!" a seaman breathed. "It's hell on earth!"

"Belay that!" Palmer said harshly. "Get a grip, Wilson. You won't be of any use to yourself or to us if you go off the deep end."

"I'm fine, sir," the seaman said.

"I hope so. For your sake."

Bolan climbed, taking the steps two at a stride. He kept the rail at his back and his eyes fixed upward. Shadowy movements swirled in the smoke. He glimpsed a few figures but not clearly enough to tell if they were friend or foe.

At a landing Bolan crouched to take his bearings. The battle had risen to a crescendo. Apparently Captain Gowen and company were giving the smugglers as good as they got.

"We'll climb three abreast," the soldier said. "Palmer and Wilson will be with me in front, and we'll keep low so the rest of you can shoot over our heads. When we see smugglers, open fire. Don't wait for my orders."

Shoulder to shoulder, they climbed. Bolan was in the middle. As they rounded the next turn a knot of hardmen appeared, racing madly to escape Captain Gowen's boarding party above.

Bolan flicked the selector lever to auto and sprayed the foremost ranks. Two dropped in their tracks. The rest halted and were promptly ripped to ribbons by the withering hailstorm loosed by Palmer and his men. Those smugglers not immediately hit backpedaled frantically.

Several bodies littered the next landing. Bolan

made sure each casualty was indeed dead before he went on. He didn't relish getting a slug between the shoulder blades.

Another group of hardmen trying to flee the carnage pounded into view. They were quick to shoot but in their haste none of their initial rounds was accurate. Bolan and the Coast Guard detail didn't let excitement spoil their aim. Riddled bodies fell like flies. When the last one was down, Bolan gestured and assumed the lead, flying up the steps. He still had several to go to reach the prone forms when one sat up, twisted and awkwardly flailed an arm at him.

It took a second for Bolan to realize the sailor held a grenade.

8

The kill radius of a hand grenade depended on the type. An M-67 fragmentation grenade would fling razor-sharp shrapnel into anyone within fifty feet of the blast. A high-explosive round for a grenade launcher would kill all those within fifteen to twenty feet, spewing more than 325 lethal fragments on detonation. An airburst grenade had an even greater kill zone.

The grenade sailing toward the Executioner appeared to be an F-1, a classic pineapple favored by the Russians and the Chinese and used by terrorists and criminal organizations worldwide. They preferred it because it had one of the largest kill zones of any grenade made, eighty feet or more.

Bolan realized that while he might be able to jump over the side before the grenade went off, there was no time for the coastguardsmen to take cover. The blast would tear them to shreds.

Bolan's only hope was the four-second fuse delay. He leaped, snagged the pineapple on the fly, wrenched to the right and hurled the bomb over the rail. "Get down!" he yelled, going prone. He was inches from the landing when the F-1 went off. The concussion seemed to lift the landing toward him. He hit hard and rolled, hearing metal scream in protest and the staccato impact of multiple fragments against the underside of the landing. A fist-sized section blew open a hand's width from his head.

It was like being caught in an earthquake.

The shaking subsided as quickly as it had begun. His eardrums aching, Bolan rose unsteadily. Thick smoke shrouded the companionway. He had no way of knowing if the landing was still intact or if it had partially buckled. "Ensign Palmer?"

"Here, sir. Wilson is hurt."

A spate of coughing drew Bolan to them. Seaman Wilson had taken several small fragments in the left leg. The flesh was badly chewed, the bone exposed. His major arteries, though, had been spared. The seaman grimaced, his teeth clenched.

The other appeared from out of the smoke, shaken and caked with dust but none the worse for wear. One of them, swatting at the smoke, suddenly raised his head. "Hey! Listen! Am I deaf, or what?"

Bolan straightened. Except for a smattering of small-arms fire, the din had died down.

"Did we win, or did they?" Palmer wondered aloud.

In answer, from above, a clipped voice called out, "Who's down there? Palmer, is that you I hear?"

The ensign jumped to his feet. "Lieutenant Hanover! Yes, sir! We have a man down, but the rest of us are fine!"

Feet drummed on the steps. The smoke began to clear, allowing Bolan to see how lucky they had been. A third of the landing was gone, rendered so much scrap. Twenty or thirty holes pockmarked the portion that remained, some of them the size of melons.

Hanover was a stocky man who looked to be as strong as a bull. He saluted Bolan, then bent to examine Wilson. Unclipping a radio from his belt, he reported in.

The reply was garbled by static but clear enough for Bolan to hear his cover name mentioned.

"Commander Belasko, the captain gives his regards," Hanover said, relaying the message. "He says that other than a few lone holdouts, the ship is secure. He's waiting for you topside. Ensign Palmer and his men are to go with you."

"I don't need a baby-sitter, Lieutenant," Bolan said, starting up.

"Captain's orders, sir. Sorry."

The main deck was a shambles, the superstructure a spidery tangle of charred girders, shattered bulkheads and ruptured decks. A dozen small fires had broken out and were being attended to. Bodies were everywhere, none of them coastguardsmen.

Captain Gowen had been wounded in the right shoulder. He was being bandaged as Bolan approached. "We did it, Commander! And miracle of miracles, we didn't lose a single soul." Gowen hiked his shoulder up and down, causing the man trying to bandage him to frown. "A few nicks here and there is all."

"Your men deserve commendations, Captain," Bolan said, and meant it. The action had been fast and furious. He was glad everything had worked out so well, but they still had one problem to deal with. "About that sub..."

"No need to remind me. As soon as butterfingers here is done, we'll transfer to the *Liberty* and go after it. Lieutenant Hanover can handle things here for a while."

Bolan stepped to the buckled rail to survey the Pacific. There was no sign of the minisub. He figured that it was still limping along, either toward San Francisco or into shore.

The captain refused to be lowered onto the cutter. He went down the way he had come up, using a rope. A cheer rose from the men on the forecastle, and he acknowledged it with a hearty salute. "You can tell your grandchildren about this night, boys!" he hollered.

The good mood lasted until they stepped onto the bridge. Bolan knew by the expression on the petty officer who greeted them that something was drastically wrong.

"Sir! We've been trying to reach you, and just contacted Lieutenant Hanover a few moments ago. We've lost the sub."

"What?" Gowen took the conn and barked out, "Sonar! I want an update on that sub!"

"It's gone sir. The unit hasn't worked right since they jammed us. I've calibrated and recalibrated, and still no trace of it."

Bolan didn't let his frustration show. If that sub reached the metro area, two tons or more of coke would flood L.A.'s streets.

Gowen was mystified. "This makes no sense. A

sub can't simply disappear unless it hides on the bottom, and that one was in no shape to dive two feet, let alone to the ocean floor.''

"Maybe they tried and sank, sir,'' someone suggested.

Bolan couldn't agree. Whatever else the smugglers might be, they weren't stupid. Whoever piloted the submersible wasn't about to commit certain suicide. There had to be a perfectly logical explanation for the sub's disappearance, and all Bolan had to do was figure out what it was.

An old adage cropped unbidden into Bolan's mind, a saying about the best place to hide always being in plain sight. "Behind the *Parismina*,'' he said.

Gowen glanced at him. "What did you say? I didn't quite catch it.''

"The only place they can be is behind the refrigerator ship. Sonar won't pick them up if they're close to its hull and have killed their engine.''

The captain nodded. "I'd bet my bottom dollar that you're right. Helm, bring us around on the other side of the *Parismina*. Petty Officer Kline, contact Lieutenant Hanover. Explain that we're swinging around to the west and I'll be in touch again shortly.''

Bolan removed the magazine from his M-16, plucked a new one from a pocket and slapped it home as the *Liberty* eased away from the refrigerator ship and made for its bow. The helmsman gave it a wide berth, then angled toward the *Parismina*'s port hull.

It was as black as the deepest cavern. No floodlights lit the scene, nor were any spotlights trained on the waterline from on high. To make matters worse, a fog bank was moving in and parts of the ship were mired in murky soup. Gowen ordered that the cutter's spotlights rake the hull from stem to stern.

A seaman on the bridge cried out, "There she is, sir! Amidships!"

All eyes fixed on the squat gray shape impaled by a spotlight beam. No figures were in sight on top of it, but there was movement, a spurt of water under the surface close to her bow.

The smugglers had launched a torpedo.

"Helm, evasive action!" Gowen roared. "Hard to starboard!"

The *Liberty* veered, but at that range there was no chance at all of evading the torpedo. A shudder ran the length of the cutter, and all hands had to grab for support to stay on their feet. Within seconds an overhead speaker blared with a damage report.

"Captain! We've taken a hit in the rudder or the prop strut. We can't maneuver."

"Damn those vermin!" Gowen raged. "They've given us a taste of our own medicine! If they fire again, we'll be blown out of the water!"

Incredibly the sub didn't press its advantage. Instead, it nosed away from the refrigerator ship, turned and headed southward.

"They don't know how crippled we are so they're making a run for it!" Gowen said. He pounded the console. "And there isn't a thing we can do to stop them. Our big gun is worthless at this close range."

It wasn't hard for Bolan to predict the sub's next move. It would scurry around to the east side of the *Parismina,* then head for the coast, keeping the big ship between it and the Coast Guard cutter. Whoever piloted that vessel knew all the ploys, and then some.

Once again Bolan had to stand by helplessly and watch as a boatload of illegal drugs was spirited right out from under his nose. Or did he? The soldier stepped over to Gowen. "You have two motor launches on board. I saw them when I came on."

"For rescue operations," Gowen said absently, more interested in the fleeing sub.

"How fast can they go?"

"Oh, fifteen to twenty knots in a calm sea. They're built to hold up under the roughest of weather, not for speed. Why do you—?" Gowen pivoted, understanding widening his eyes. "It just might work! That sub can't be doing any better than fifteen knots. I'll send a detail along."

"No," Bolan said, unwilling to brook an argument. This was one job he had to do alone. Added weight would only slow him. Plus he didn't want to be saddled with having to safeguard the coastguardsmen. Life-and-death risks were better taken alone. "And that's final."

The captain hesitated.

"You were told to cooperate fully with me," Bolan bluntly reminded him. "Will you or won't you?"

Three minutes later Bolan was being lowered into the motor launch, which bobbed on the water beside the cutter. He lost no time in turning over the outboard and revving into top speed, his wake washing up against the *Parismina* as he raced around the ship and took off after the sub.

The fog had grown thicker. Locating the vessel would be a hopeless task if not for the radio Gowen had given him. Bolan switched it on and pressed the red button to transmit. "*Liberty,* this is Commander Belasko. Is sonar picking up the sub?"

The captain answered. "Off and on. The unit is still on the fritz. As near as we can tell, it's bearing to the northeast at twelve knots."

"Roger." Bolan placed the radio on the seat and hunched forward. A constant fine spray drenched him. Combined with the clammy fog, he was chilled to the bone in no time even though the temperature had to be in the sixties. Relying on a compass, he headed in the same direction as the sub.

The soldier looked back once, but the *Parismina* had been swallowed by the thick bank of fog. He couldn't see more than a dozen yards into the dank gloom, if that.

The bobbing rhythm of the launch was hypnotic. Bolan found his mind drifting and shook his head to clear it. Other than the slapping of the waves and the rumble of the motor, there were no other sounds. It was as if he was alone in the world, the sole speck of life on a limitless sea. Then, faintly in the distance, a foghorn sounded.

Bolan picked up the radio. "*Liberty,* Belasko. Are there any other ships in our area?"

After a few seconds, Gowen answered. "We can't

say for sure. Our radar has gone completely haywire. But the last we knew, no.''

The soldier thanked him and set the radio at his side, then fixed his gaze to the compass needle. Provided the sub didn't change its heading, he should overtake it before the smugglers reached shore.

Moments later the wind gusted so hard that the launch swerved off course. Bolan compensated. No sooner did he do so than a second gust did the same. It also roiled the fog, reducing visibility even more. He grasped the steering arm with both hands and locked his elbows to prevent being blown astray a third time.

After several minutes Bolan decided to raise the *Liberty* again on the off chance they had their sonar on-line. It was imperative that he learn whether the sub had deviated from its original bearing. Repeated tries were rewarded with nothing but static. Since he wasn't out of range, he had to conclude the radio or the incoming weather system was to blame. Either way, he was on his own in more ways than one.

A short time later the wind died, and the fog tapered off to infrequent patches. Bolan took that as a good sign until he looked up to confirm his bearings by the stars and saw a charcoal slate of clouds. At the same moment, raindrops began to fall, only a few at first but growing in number and size rapidly. A storm was just what he needed.

Bolan opened the throttle the last degree. The wind increased again, stronger than ever, battering the small launch relentlessly. It took all of the soldier's strength to maintain his hold on the steering arm.

A blast of cold air struck the launch with the impact of a hurricane. The bow danced and weaved as Bolan fought to stay on course. Heavier drops of rain pelted him. He had to squint to see, and even then he couldn't see much farther than he had been able to in the heavy fog. That changed for the worse when the storm broke in earnest.

A sheet of pounding rain cut visibility to zero. The launch swerved, tilted, nearly capsized. Waves formerly no more than a foot high reared to five times that height and tossed the launch about as if it were their personal plaything.

Bolan still believed he would be all right as long as the outboard engine didn't conk out on him. Plowing on, he was buffeted as if by unseen hands. The wind howled like a banshee, shrieking so loudly that he could barely hear the engine above the tempest.

The bow swung eastward and wouldn't be turned. Bolan's only consolation was that the storm pushed him toward the coast, not out to sea.

Bolan tried in vain to get the launch to go in the direction he wanted. In another minute the engine sputtered and coughed, wheezing like someone taking his last few breaths. He adjusted the throttle, but it did no good. The sputtering grew worse.

Predictably the engine died. Bolan attempted to start it again, without success.

The storm, which had been growing stronger, picked that moment to unleash its full elemental fury. Hurricane-force winds tossed the small boat about. The rain drove at Bolan as hard as hail. Towering waves lifted the craft as easily as if it were made of paper and flung it every which way.

All Bolan could do was hold on tight and hope he was still in one piece when the launch struck land. Like a bobbing cork in a whirlpool, the boat bounced, swayed and spun, nearly making him dizzy with its mad gyrations.

He glimpsed a wave bigger than any he had yet seen sweep toward him out of the gloom. Under him, the boat shook violently, then was flung toward the sky as if striving to get airborne. An instant later the launch plummeted.

Another wave reared overhead. Bolan felt sure it would crash down on top of him and tear him loose, but the boat was instead lifted again and twirled around so many times that he could no longer tell in which direction the coastline lay.

Suddenly the launch tilted sharply. The radio went flying into the water. Bolan had to wrap his arms and legs around the seat to keep from joining it. Cold water cascaded over him, soaking whatever few square inches of skin hadn't already been drenched. Salt water got into his ears, his nose, even his mouth.

Just when Bolan thought the launch would capsize, it righted itself and rushed on into the night, carried by a series of waves so enormous they dwarfed the boat. Without warning, the vessel listed once more. Bolan was thrown against the bow and managed to grab the gunwale to keep from going over. Another toss sent him careening aft. His left arm snagged a seat, but in doing so it was nearly torn from the socket. He gripped the seat with both hands and felt something bump against his side.

It was the M-16. The sling had been jarred off his shoulder and hung down near his wrist. He couldn't let go to slide it up again or he might find himself in the raging sea, where he wouldn't last two seconds.

The wind roared louder than a jet engine, so loud it nearly drowned out the hammering rain and the roaring waves. So loud that at first Bolan didn't detect a new sound in the distance, a sound that meant the worst danger was yet to come.

Repeated loud booms echoed across the turbulent ocean, broken now and again by a sibilant hissing such as a gigantic snake might utter. Only an oversize serpent wasn't responsible. What Bolan heard was the unmistakable crash of high waves on offshore reefs. And the launch appeared to be headed right for them.

The booming became louder by the moment. Bolan pressed back against the transom and coiled his legs under him. Peering intently ahead, he saw white spray being flung into the air by waves dashing on massive rocks. Only the crowns of the rocks were visible, barely so.

The launch was lifted high, and something scraped the bottom. Bolan tensed for a crash that never came. He was jolted as the boat smacked down again but grateful it hadn't been reduced to splinters. His relief, though, proved premature.

Materializing as if from nowhere, another rock speared out of the water, about to impale the launch.

At the last possible moment, the craft swerved, swept by a wave into a wide pocket nestled between five or six ragged rocks, any one of which was large enough to destroy the launch.

Here the waves couldn't reach. The wind wasn't as strong. But the boat was still buffeted, first in one direction, then in another. It cracked against a rock to the left, swung about and grated against another to the right. Bolan saw a gap wide enough for the launch to pass through. Unfortunately he had no way of reaching it.

For harrowing minutes the boat was thrown about, flung against rock after rock, but never at the gap. He came close once, and leaned over the side to paddle in an effort to shoot out of the pocket. Nature had other ideas. The next wave to strike the outer rocks created an eddy that swirled the boat away from the opening.

Bolan knew it was only a matter of time before the launch sprang a leak or broke up entirely. No boat could long withstand the battering it was taking. If it sank there in that pocket, he might never make it out. Tidal suction could pull him under, or he might be flung against a rock so hard that it killed him.

Ominous rumbling drew Bolan's gaze seaward. No obvious explanation was evident, not until a few seconds went by and he distinguished an immense swell rushing headlong toward the reef. It was larger than any single wave.

Whirling, Bolan flung himself from the launch in a desperate bid to reach the opening. He was still in midair when a solid wall of water enclosed him in its grip. There was no resisting it; there was no breaking free. Bolan felt himself thrust aloft. Pressure from behind tumbled him head over heels, again and again. Something gouged into his stomach, and he almost opened his mouth in a reflexive gasp.

A span of seconds seemed like an eternity. The swell broke around him in a band of bubbling froth. Bolan was spilled forward by his own momentum. He tumbled a dozen feet, then came to a stop. Straightening, he broke the surface and trod water to catch his breath. He never got the chance.

A wave smashed over him, nearly bowling Bolan over. Coughing out seawater he had inadvertently swallowed, the soldier began to swim, heading in the direction the wave had been going, since that was where the shore was likely to be. There was no way of knowing how far off it was. He swam and swam, pumping his arms and legs, resisting the pull of the undertow and the waves that slammed into him every few seconds. Bit by bit the tremendous exertion took a toll. He could feel his strength ebbing. His limbs became leaden. Gritting his teeth, he kept going, refusing to give up while a spark of life remained.

The Executioner was on the brink of total exhaustion when one last wave seized him and hurled him forward as if he were a human javelin. His shoulder hit something hard. His knees and elbows banged on solid ground. Barely able to think, let alone move, he somehow found the energy to propel himself a few yards farther. It was his last act before a black veil claimed him.

9

The raucous cries of gulls brought the Executioner into consciousness. He got to his knees, half expecting to be swamped by another enormous wave, only to find that it was broad daylight and he was on a sandy beach twenty yards from the water. He squinted in the bright sunshine, checking his watch. The new day was less than an hour old.

Bolan took stock. His clothes were damp but not as wet as they had been. The M-16 was gone, as was his Beretta. Thankfully the Desert Eagle hadn't been torn from the holster on his right hip. And he still had plenty of lethal tools in the pockets of his blacksuit.

He slowly rose. His body felt as if he had been battered from head to toe by a blackjack, and his left leg bore a nasty gash. He shook his arms to loosen the tense muscles while surveying the vicinity.

It was a deserted cove. On the left reared a cliff, and on the right a spine of land linked to a tract of dense forest. Not another living soul was anywhere to be seen.

In addition to the gulls, crabs scuttled at the water's edge. Nearby was part of the shattered wreck of the motor launch. It was the stern section, badly crumpled and lacking the outboard motor, which evidently had been ripped off and was resting somewhere on the bottom of the cove.

Off to the right lay another large piece. The soldier passed it on the way to the spine, which he scaled by following a ribbon of a hiking trail to the top. From the crown he hoped to be able to see far out to sea. If he could spot the *Parismina,* he would be able to get his bearings.

The refrigerator ship wasn't anywhere in sight. Bolan scoured the ocean thoroughly, yet the only vessel he saw was a sailboat on the horizon. It wasn't hard to understand why. The storm had driven him well off his original heading.

The main issue for Bolan to decide was whether he had been driven to the south or the north. Based on the prevailing winds, he reasoned that it had been the former. The quickest way to reach civilization so he could put in a phone call to Brognola was to continue northward until he came to a town. With that in mind, he started over the rim of the narrow ridge, then drew up short in surprise.

Beyond lay another, larger cove. Bordered by trees that grew thickly right down to its sandy beach, the water was dotted with boulders the size of a small house and many smaller monoliths. No ship could possibly pass through them and reach the shore in safety.

The minisub, though, had tried.

Bolan rested his hand on the butt of the Desert Eagle when he saw the crippled submersible lying on its side, half in and half out of the water. He could also see footprints in the moist sand. Seeking cover, he warily worked his way lower until he was among small boulders that lined the base of the spine.

As near as Bolan could tell, no one was outside the sub. But the tracks were ample proof that at least one smuggler had survived the tempest and had to be either in the vessel or in the trees. Either way, Bolan invited a hail of lead if he showed himself.

The rocks were slick and treacherous. An added complication, thanks to the storm, came in the form of scores of large crabs that had been washed onto the beach. Some had pincers as big, or bigger, than Bolan's hands. Every step he took, he had to be careful not to tread on one. When he gripped rocks, he had to be sure he didn't accidentally place a hand in the wrong spot or he risked losing a finger.

Bolan carefully picked his way to a point forty yards from the sub. As he got closer, the damage inflicted by the elements became apparent. The hull had been breached on the top and the port side. There was also an uneven hole below the conning tower large enough for a man to crawl through. The propeller was a crumpled wreck, the rudder mangled beyond recognition. It was amazing the vessel had made it as far as it had.

Coming to the last cluster of rocks, Bolan put his hand on one to lean out for another glimpse of the footprints. Almost too late, he was aware of movement under his palm. He snatched his hand back as a mammoth crab's pincer snapped within half an inch of his little finger.

Bolan wedged the barrel of the Desert Eagle under

the crustacean and flicked. He intended for the crab to fall quietly at the bottom of the rock, but its wildly waving legs caught on the edge and it pushed off into the sea, hitting with a loud splash.

The soldier promptly ducked. He listened for voices and footsteps but heard neither. Waiting a suitable interval, he poked his head out again.

The sound hadn't drawn any triggermen. Standing, Bolan padded toward the sub. He swung the .44 Magnum pistol from side to side, ready to fall into a Weaver stance at the first sign of a gunner. None showed.

Silence enveloped the submarine. The hatch was wide open, and beneath it a series of tracks led away from the vessel. Also present were scuff marks where heavy objects had been lowered, then dragged off into the forest.

Bolan sank onto one knee to peer inside. A few lights were on, but they flickered. He tried to incite a response by smacking his hand against the hull a few times. Nothing happened.

The idea of going inside didn't appeal to him. In the cramped confines he would be at the mercy of anyone who might be covering the ladder. As he sat looking at the vessel, he noticed a patch of white close to the hatch. Reaching out, he palmed a transparent packet filled with white powder.

Cocaine.

That explained the scuff marks. Bolan set the packet back in the conning tower and made for the trees. The tracks overlapped, so it was hard to gauge exactly how many smugglers had survived the storm.

Once under the canopy of branches, he came on a trail of crushed grass and weeds that bore off in a northeasterly direction.

Holstering the Desert Eagle, Bolan started out in pursuit at a slow jog. He paced himself in order not to tire too soon. The shoreline was hilly and covered with verdant growth. It made for rough going, but it also meant that the smugglers had it rougher. They were fleeing with hundreds of pounds of cocaine, which was bound to slow them.

About a quarter of a mile from the Pacific, Bolan crested a knoll. To his right, high weeds had been trampled. He veered to check why and discovered an earthen mound crudely covered with vegetation to hide it from prying aerial eyes.

A broken branch served as a hastily improvised shovel. Bolan scooped until he exposed a large cache of white packets. As much as he wanted to destroy the stash, he covered it up and went on. An explosion or smoke might alert the smugglers. Brognola's people would see to it that the cocaine was properly disposed of.

The Executioner pushed himself to go faster. A steep slope brought him to a small marsh rife with reeds. The smugglers had gone straight across, so he did the same, wading into waist-deep water.

Bolan was two-thirds of the way across when a shot rang out. At the same split second, a geyser erupted next to his left leg. He bounded to the right, to one of many tiny islets of solid ground in the middle of the marsh. As he crouched, another slug thudded into the dank earth.

The Desert Eagle filled his fist. Holding his fire until he pinpointed the shooter, Bolan craned his neck. The shots had come from a hill due east. Choked with brush and weeds, it offered enough hiding places to shield an entire platoon.

One of the oldest ruses in the book was called for. Bolan broke a short branch off a sturdy bush, held it at the bottom and elevated it above the islet, slowly swinging his arm back and forth.

The crack of a pistol was the soldier's reward. Several leaves dissolved, raining onto his shoulders. He tossed the branch aside and studied a shelf halfway up the slope. The gunner was there, lying in tall grass.

Bolan wondered why only one smuggler was taking shots at him. The logical conclusion was that the rest had gone on, leaving their companion to make sure they got away. Maybe, Bolan mused, they had spotted him from a long way off, perhaps with binoculars.

Of more pressing concern was the fact the shots would alert the smugglers up ahead. Bolan had to outflank the gunner and hurry on. To that end he abruptly took two steps to the left, deliberately exposing himself. Then, spinning, he bolted to the right just as another shot rang out. Only this time, instead of ducking behind the islet, he raced past it toward the growth that fringed the marsh to the south.

The shooter took a few seconds to compensate. Bolan covered ten feet, fifteen. He zigzagged just as the fourth blast sounded. The slug splatted into the water behind him. Weaving, he passed another stump of land, which absorbed the fifth round.

Cutting to the right, Bolan sped toward a tree and gained sanctuary without being fired on again. The big .44 in his right hand, he immediately plunged into the vegetation.

Caution was sacrificed for speed. Bolan's goal was to reach the hill before the gunner slipped away. He paused when he reached his objective, but only long enough to scan the shelf and ensure the gunner didn't have him lined up in cross hairs.

Swinging around to the east side of the hill, Bolan climbed. He was shy of the rim when a grunting sound brought him to a stop. The grunt was repeated, along with a scraping sound. Flattening, the soldier rolled behind a pine and waited.

Huffing and puffing replaced the grunting. A hand appeared, holding an Astra A-70, then a sweaty head framed by brown hair and a clipped beard. Pain showing on his face, the man crawled over the top and stopped to catch his breath.

Bolan saw that he had been wrong. The smugglers hadn't left one of their number behind just to ambush him. The man was there because he couldn't go any farther. His left leg had been crushed from the knee down. It looked as if the limb had been pinned under a steamroller. Pale bone and mangled flesh showed through shredded jeans.

The smuggler slid to a boulder and rose with his back propped against it. Putting the 9 mm pistol in his lap, he wiped a hand across his forehead and closed his eyes.

It was the opening Bolan needed. Taking three swift strides, he positioned himself to the right of the gunner, leveled the Desert Eagle and thumbed back the hammer.

At the distinct click, the man stiffened and shifted. He started to grab for his pistol but froze with his fingers brushing the butt.

"I wouldn't if I were you," Bolan said.

The smuggler wet his lips. "Pretty slick, mister."

"Put your hands behind your head and don't move." After the man complied, Bolan advanced and took the Astra. He stuck it under his belt, then stepped back. "You have a name?"

"Griffin. Tom Griffin."

Bolan nodded at the leg. "Did that happen on the sub?"

Griffin, scowling, nodded. "Damn that rotten storm! We were tossed around like sardines in a tin can. A bank of equipment fell on top of me."

"How many are up ahead?"

The smuggler smirked. "Funny thing. All that bumping around rattled my brain something fierce. I can't seem to remember."

"No matter," Bolan said, backing off. The stricken man wasn't going anywhere. He could leave Griffin there for Brognola's people to pick up when they came for the sub.

"Hold on there! Not so fast. You can't just up and leave me like this. I need medical attention. You have to take me to the closest hospital before it's too late."

"Nice try," Bolan said, "but you brought this on

yourself. I'll contact someone about coming to get you as soon as I reach a phone." He started to turn but halted when Griffin called out.

"I'm begging you, mister! I hurt so bad, I can barely think straight! Those heartless bastards I called my friends left me here to die. They were afraid I'd slow them down."

"I'll put in a call," Bolan promised, which was the best he could do under the circumstances.

Griffin doubled over, his arms pressed to his stomach, and groaned. "Please!" he begged. "I'll be dead by the time anyone shows up!" His hand slipped under the beige jacket he wore.

Bolan pointed the Desert Eagle. "Don't try it," he advised. "Raise your hands where I can see them."

"No can do, big guy," Griffin stated. "I promised my buddies that I'd waste your sorry ass, and that's exactly what I'm going to do." With that, he flicked his arm out from under the jacket. Glinting in his left hand was another Astra.

Bolan had to stroke the big .44's trigger only once. Fueled by 240 grains of powder, the jacketed hollow-point exploded from the muzzle at a velocity of 1300 feet per second. It shattered Griffin's sternum, sheared through his internal organs and burst out his back next to his spine, leaving a hole the size of an apple.

The smuggler's eyes fluttered, and he keeled forward, his fingers going limp.

Bolan claimed the second pistol, then hastened eastward, down the hill to a flat field dotted with puddles from the heavy rain. Three sets of tracks were clearly imprinted in the mud, telling the soldier how many people he was up against.

The field ended at a wide thicket. To skirt the barrier, the smugglers had gone around to the north.

Choosing a more direct route, Bolan followed a game trail into the heart of the growth. The trail was barely wide enough, but he used it anyway, heedless of the thorns and branches that gouged his shoulders and forearms.

The shortcut paid off. Bolan emerged from the other side and found the smugglers' trail. He had gained a couple of minutes on them, and every one counted.

Now the soldier adopted a new tactic. Rather than stick to the trail, he veered into the brush and paralleled the tracks. It was a necessary precaution in the event another hardman was lying in wait.

For more than half a mile nothing happened. Bolan was constantly on the lookout for the three smugglers. Their trail wound into a maze of manzanita, forcing him to move closer to it to keep their tracks in sight. He had penetrated twenty or thirty feet when he noticed something that brought him to an abrupt halt.

Birds sang merrily to the north and south of the manzanita. But in the manzanita itself, it was as quiet as a graveyard. That shouldn't be, Bolan told himself. The smugglers had gone by at least fifteen minutes earlier, maybe longer. There should be birds near where he stood, yet not so much as an insect stirred.

Bolan went on, at half the pace as before. The Desert Eagle was nestled in his palm, his finger curled around the trigger. He ducked to go under a low limb, and the movement saved his life.

A metal firestorm blistered the limb, chewing it into so much kindling that rained on Bolan's head and shoulders as he dived. Flipping behind a narrow trunk, he probed the thick stand. Whoever was after him had to be using an SMG. Adding to the gunner's advantage, the SMG had been fitted with a sound suppressor.

Bolan had no way of pinpointing exactly where the shots came from. One thing was for certain, however—he couldn't stay where he was. The shooter would be jockeying for a better position, so the soldier had to get out of there before the man found it.

In a sinuous crawl Bolan headed to the south. After crossing the trail, he turned east, staying flat against the ground. Amid a circular patch of yellow flowers he stopped and slightly elevated his eyes. No hardmen were anywhere in sight.

Biding his time, Bolan's interest perked when a pair of finches took excited wing from a manzanita about forty feet to the northeast of where he had been standing when the smuggler opened fire. A couple of low limbs moved, then a large bald head appeared.

Bolan sighted quickly, but not quickly enough. The black man dropped from sight. No rustling branches or quivering leaves betrayed which direction he went. The man knew his stuff.

Snaking onward until he deemed it safe, Bolan rose behind a sheltering tree. It occurred to him that the bald smuggler was purposely slowing him so the remaining pair could get away. Knowing it didn't change anything. He couldn't go on and leave the gunner at his back. He had to drop the man then and there.

Bolan looped to the north. Soon a faintly acrid scent drew him to three crushed cigarettes that marked where the man had been waiting for him. A few yards to the north lay spent casings.

They were 7.76 mm rounds, a caliber in which submachine guns were rarely manufactured. So rare, that Bolan had a good idea the weapon was an M-61 Skorpion, a Czech-made machine pistol widely distributed among terrorist organizations and other criminal elements. Despite the underpowered cartridge, it was an excellent weapon for illicit use because it was so small and could be easily concealed, and it could be silenced with a suppressor half as long as most currently in use.

The Skorpion had another drawback in addition to the caliber. Only two magazines were available, 10- and 20-round box types. Compared to the 30- to 40-round magazines more common among subguns and machine pistols, it limited the shooter's firepower. The best way to trigger the Skorpion was to employ short bursts so as to conserve ammo, a knack developed only after considerable practice. Based on the limb that had been shot to ribbons, the smuggler hadn't used the SMG often.

Still, as always, the Executioner took nothing for granted. As vigilant as a hawk, he tracked the man who was stalking him. Boot prints steered him to the place the smuggler had been standing when Bolan glimpsed the man's head. From there the prints made a circuitous approach to where Bolan had been when the smuggler shot at him.

The smuggler had gone south, on the soldier's path. Bolan looked for sign of the man among the dappled shadows. Finding none, he rose and sprinted across the original trail.

Bolan came to the circle of yellow flowers. He went around them this time rather than through them, and he was about to duck into the manzanitas again when he spotted a green backpack a few yards to his right.

Hugging the earth, Bolan braced for shots that never came. The pack had to be bait, he suspected, left to lure him into the open. Yet try as he might, he couldn't locate the smuggler's hiding place.

The game of cat and mouse had gone on long enough. Every moment Bolan was delayed gave the other pair that much more time to reach a highway and hitch a ride. Once they did, there would be no catching them. So Bolan decided to bring matters to a head. Backing into brush, he collected a handful of small stones. The first he threw at the pack. It hit loudly enough but provoked no response. He tossed a second stone into the manzanitas flanking it, with the same result.

A third throw into the trees south of the flowers finally elicited a reaction, although not the one Bolan had counted on. A rustled sound behind him grabbed his attention. He glanced over his right shoulder and saw the smuggler taking aim with the Skorpion.

Only, instead of focusing on any of the spots where Bolan had tossed rocks, the smuggler was taking aim at the Executioner. His ploy had backfired.

The gunner sneered and fired.

10

It was the sneer that saved the Executioner's life. If the smuggler had simply pressed the trigger the moment their eyes made contact, he would have stitched Bolan from neck to thigh. But the man indulged in a caustic sneer of triumph, a twitch of the mouth that took no more than a second. That second, though, was all the Executioner needed to hurtle into a roll that brought him up in a combat crouch with the Desert Eagle aligned for instantaneous target acquisition.

The big .44 did just that as slugs from the Skorpion made a patchwork tapestry of dots in the soil where Bolan had just been. Twice the big .44 rocked, the heavy rounds punching the smuggler high on the chest, spinning him. The SMG clattered as he sagged onto his knees, then melted to the ground. Not once did the smuggler speak or cry out in pain.

Covering the shooter, Bolan walked forward to press a thumb against a pulse in the man's neck and confirm the kill. Since time was crucial, he added the Skorpion to his growing arsenal and trotted in pursuit of the final pair.

Time was more crucial than ever. The delays had

given the smugglers a good lead, and Bolan resigned himself to the fact that they might elude him.

The land climbed, not steeply but steadily. The trees thinned. Bolan broke into the open and spied more woodland a few hundred yards away and two running figures sprinting toward it. He poured on the speed, no longer caring if they saw him. They knew he was after them. Using stealth would only slow him.

Halfway across the open strip, Bolan tensed as the blast of a car horn sounded in the distance. A highway wasn't far off, and the pair could flag a ride.

As Bolan neared the woodland, he caught sight of several picnic tables and benches. The smugglers had blundered into a small public park, one of dozens that lined the Pacific Coast. Innocent bystanders were at risk of being injured.

Almost on cue, a family of four appeared. The parents carried a cooler and basket, the kids arguing over who got to play with a rubber ball.

Bolan lowered the Skorpion to his side so it wouldn't be obvious. He also pulled his black shirt out from under the top of his pants and draped it over the two Astras and the butt of the Desert Eagle. That was the best he could do. Just in time, too. The father and mother glanced at him but displayed no alarm.

Buildings were visible through the trees. Rest rooms were on the left, an information center on the right. Only four cars occupied the parking lot, and only a few people were nearby.

A few was still too many. Bolan slowed, trying to

guess which way the smugglers had gone. Two women emerged from the building on the left. He might not have given them a second look if their clothes hadn't been so rumpled and sweaty, and if they weren't carrying backpacks exactly like the one the black smuggler had been toting.

Bolan stepped behind a pine. Neither of the women was taller than five feet two or so, and both were stocky. They also wore their hair in matching cuts. They were similar enough to be twins, except one had red hair and the other black. Mopping their faces with damp paper towels, they strode to a water fountain, set down their packs and indulged in long drinks. When they finished, a young mother and her child came over to drink.

Bolan couldn't do anything. He frowned when another car, with out-of-state plates, rolled into the lot and braked close to the fountain. Two men got out, stretched, then ambled toward the information center.

The women huddled, the redhead pointing at the sedan. They watched the two men closely, and the moment the tourists were inside, the women grabbed their heavy packs and hustled to the vehicle.

Bolan could guess why. The trusting tourists had left the key in the ignition. Breaking from cover, he sprinted across the parking lot. The women were so intent on stealing the car that they might not notice him until he was right on them.

But it wouldn't prove to be that easy.

The young mother and child had turned from the fountain and were walking toward the trees. It was the mother who noticed the Executioner, recoiled and called out anxiously, "Hey! Is that a gun you've got there?"

The stocky smugglers heard. The redhead was closer, on the driver's side. She had the door open and was lifting a leg to slide in. The raven-haired woman was about to do the same on the passenger side, and both swiveled at the yell.

In Bolan's line of work, he didn't have the luxury of making distinctions between men and women. He could never treat the so-called fairer sex any differently than he could a typical triggerman. In combat, a female gunner was every bit as deadly as her male counterpart.

So when the redhead's hand flashed from under her blouse holding a pistol, Bolan did as he would have done with a male shooter. He snapped the Skorpion into a two-handed grip and drilled a burst into the woman's chest, as bystanders fled in panic.

The redhead's partner was the only one who didn't lose her head. As the redhead jerked from the multiple impacts, the black haired smuggler sprawled across the front seat, twisted the ignition and revved the engine. She had to back up to get out of there, and in throwing the car into reverse, she brought it nearer to Bolan.

Since the Skorpion had cycled empty, Bolan tossed it aside. He started to draw the Desert Eagle just as the smuggler threw the vehicle into Drive and ducked so low in the seat that he couldn't see her. The sedan shot forward. Taking three long strides, Bolan leaped and caught hold of the lower edge of the driver's window.

"Bastard!" the woman hissed, punching at his hands.

Hanging on for all he was worth, his shins and shoes scraping over the hard asphalt, the soldier retaliated with a right cross to her jaw that knocked her onto the seat. She lost her grip on the steering wheel. Out of control, the car slewed to the edge of the road.

Through the opposite window Bolan saw trees rush to meet them. He flung himself backward, hit and tumbled, coming to rest on his stomach as a tremendous crash rent the muggy air.

The car had plowed over a sapling, struck a pine and turned onto its side, sliding ten or fifteen feet before it came to rest against the sturdy trunk of an oak.

Palming the Desert Eagle, Bolan raced to the vehicle. The pungent odor of gasoline alerted him to fuel leaking from the gas tank. The undercarriage was hot to the touch, and it wouldn't be long before the whole thing went up.

Jumping, Bolan gripped the lower edge of the rocker panel and pulled himself up onto the door. The windshield had shattered, showering glass inside. The driver was lying in an unconscious heap at the bottom, her body crumpled partly under the dash and partly on top of the other door. A nasty gash on her brow dribbled scarlet drops.

Loud hissing issued from the undercarriage as Bolan slid in through the open window. He dropped, spreading his legs so his feet thudded down on either side of the smuggler. She was so much dead weight that he had to try twice before he lifted her onto a shoulder.

Now came the hard part, getting back out again. Bolan grasped the steering wheel and pulled himself toward the open window. Sheer force of will raised him as high as the steering column. But the woman's weight limited his reach, and he couldn't quite grab the window frame.

Meanwhile the hissing outside grew louder. Bolan envisioned the vehicle going up in a blast of molten fire. He lunged upward, snared the window and began to pull the two of them to safety.

The smuggler picked that moment to come around. She cracked her eyes open, and on seeing the soldier, she tore into him.

It was all he could do to duck his chin and let his scalp absorb most of her fury. When she went for his eyes, he tucked his chin to his chest to ward her off.

"You're not taking me in!" she declared, drawing back her arms with her hands entwined.

"I won't have to if the fuel tank goes up," Bolan said, and sniffed to dramatize his point. Despite herself, she imitated him. Suddenly shoving, she scrambled for the opening. He was right behind her. But as she clambered up onto the outer surface of the door, she whirled and kicked at his face.

Twisting, Bolan took the blow on his jaw. It drove him back against the steering wheel, but he was able to hold on to the edge of the window. Exerting every muscle in his shoulders, he heaved upward again, only to be met by her foot. Grasping it, Bolan wrenched.

The smuggler yelped, then tugged on her leg to break free. Bolan used her own leverage against her and pushed at the same instant. Before she could help herself, the woman pitched over the side.

A serpentine hiss and tendrils of smoke were ample hints that time was short. Bolan heaved up onto the door, slid and pushed off. He saw the woman scrambling to her feet, fleeing like a frightened rabbit. Grass and weeds cushioned his fall and he was erect in a flash. Instead of going in the same direction she had, he ran around the front of the sedan, knowing that when the tank blew, the body of the car would act as a buffer.

The explosion proved him right. Searing flame and heat buffeted the Executioner, but not nearly as much as enveloped the smuggler. The vehicle canted skyward, buckling. Metal shards and other debris zinged like buckshot.

Bolan threw himself onto his belly. There was nothing else he could do except fling both arms over his head and wait out the rain of flaming car parts that peppered the ground around him. One glanced off his shoulder, inflicting no real damage. The stench of burned rubber and upholstery was nauseating.

It seemed longer, but in a matter of seconds the fiery rain tapered off. Bolan was erect before the last few pieces crashed to earth. Rushing toward the parking lot, he stopped when he saw the pathetic figure sprawled near the road. The woman was charred in places. What little remained of her clothes hung in blackened tatters. Her days of smuggling cocaine were over, forever.

NESTLED IN THE SCENIC Blue Ridge Mountains of Virginia, Stony Man Farm was known only to a few people in the very highest circles of American government. Rightly labeled the nerve center of the most elite commandos in the world, Stony Man Farm was where Mack Bolan sometimes stayed between missions.

Bolan was under no obligation to accept a mission offered by Hal Brognola. Unlike most of the special operatives who worked out of the Farm, the Executioner maintained an arm's-length relationship with the U.S. government. He need only accept those assignments that appealed to him, no questions asked.

The soldier had always been his own man. In Vietnam, during his long war on the Mob and now in the middle of his personal campaign against the drug trade and terrorism, he fought the good war *his* way, not the way others might see fit.

Stopping Estavan Quesada had become a priority in that war.

After several hours of sleep, Bolan shaved and showered and made his way to the spacious dining area. It was an hour or so before dawn, the quiet hour at Stony Man when the day crew hadn't yet arrived and the night shift was winding down after eight hours of hard work. He pretty much had the dining room to himself.

Hal Brognola slid into a chair across from Bolan and smiled wearily. "How are you feeling?"

"Hungry."

"You know what I mean. I've gone over the preliminaries from all those involved. You went through a lot in the gulf, and worse out in California. Anyone else, and I'd insist they take a month's R and R."

"I'm fine," Bolan assured his friend. "Anything new on the Cat?"

"Satellite recon established that the *Cartagena* sailed through the Panama Canal and down the South American coast to Buenaventura."

Bolan rated that as good news. Buenaventura was a leading Colombian port.

"But," the big Fed went on, "nothing has happened since. The Colombians have the vessel under twenty-four-hour surveillance, and so far the only activity has been the unloading of the legal freight the ship picked up in Florida." He paused. "Our best guess is that the minisub is still on board."

"So we twiddle our thumbs until the smugglers make a move?"

"It's not by choice, believe me. But these things can take time. You know that. Colombia is a sovereign power. We can't send in the Marines, so to speak, unless we get their permission first. I've been on the phone with my opposite number at their end, a Colonel Miguel Contillo. He assures me that as soon as something develops, we'll be the first to know."

Bolan didn't mean to put his friend on the defensive, but he regarded downtime, as it was known around the Farm, as largely a waste of time. He'd much rather be out in the field, doing something, than be stuck there until word came down the pipeline.

Brognola grinned. "I see that look on your face. Well, don't worry. I'll try my best to arrange things so you're not bored to tears." The big Fed consulted his watch. "In an hour, if you're willing, meet with Cowboy in the War Room. He has something that you might find of use."

Further talk was cut short by the arrival of Bolan's breakfast.

Brognola poured a cup of coffee from a service on a side board, made small talk about the most recent Able Team mission, then hustled out to place a call to Colonel Contillo.

After finishing his meal, Bolan headed for the basement level. He took the stairs, rounding a corner and following a corridor past the gun room and several offices until he came to a steel coded access door. Punching in the proper code, he strolled into the War Room.

John "Cowboy" Kissinger was a specialist in the design of armament, and he had proved invaluable to the commandos at Stony Man on many occasions.

A number of items were on the table beside Kissinger. Some Bolan recognized, such as a wet suit and scuba gear, and a few he didn't. He nodded as the weaponsmith greeted him.

"Jack tells me that you've been trying to set a new world record for holding a breath under water."

Bolan couldn't help but grin. "Not by choice. It was either stay under or sleep with the fishes."

"Figured as much." Kissinger picked up an object

that resembled a scuba mouthpiece, only it sported small oval attachments at both ends. "Ever seen one of these?" he asked, and went on before Bolan could answer. "It's just out. It's called the Dolphina, but don't let the name fool you. With one of these babies, you can stay under for almost half an hour with no external tanks."

To demonstrate, Kissinger wedged the unit into his mouth, adjusted a tiny control knob at the bottom and breathed slowly but noisily. Taking out the mouthpiece, he said, "The key is to regulate your breathing. The slower you do it, the longer the air lasts."

"I could have used a crate of them in the gulf."

"How about one of these?" Kissinger lifted a peculiar pistol with a cloverleaf-shaped barrel. "It's the latest in underwater ordnance. We can thank the geniuses at Heckler & Koch for developing it. They call it the P-11 ZUB. It fires five lethal darts, both above the surface and below, and it's damn accurate—deadly up to ninety feet on land, about half that underwater."

The practical applications were obvious. Bolan studied the unique barrel unit. Waterproof seals covered the darts until they were triggered. "I'll take one with me when I head for Colombia. If I get the word to go, that is."

Hal Brognola chuckled behind them. He waved a paper. "Oh, ye of little faith! Pack your bags, Striker. And don't forget your sunblock lotion. Colombia can be hot as hell at this time of year."

11

The big break had come about quite by accident.

The computer room was on the first floor of the main building at Stony Man Farm. Some of the top people in the field of cybernetics worked there. Daily they were assigned to sort intelligence, access data, correlate and interpolate statistics and generally perform a thousand and one tasks essential to safeguarding the country they so proudly served.

As with any computer operation, files were kept of all pertinent information. A young woman about to file the enhanced satellite photos of the *Cartagena* happened to notice a vague dark speck on the lower edge of one photo, a speck she mistook for dust and tried to brush off.

When she realized it was ingrained into the picture, it nudged her curiosity enough for her to study the smudge under a magnifying glass. It revealed nothing. The mark might have been a whale, for all she knew, or simply have been caused during processing of the film.

Most any other clerk would have filed the photo and gone on about his or her business. But this particular young woman had no desire to spend the rest of her career filing intel day in and day out. She craved more-meaningful assignments.

To earn a promotion, she was always looking for ways to impress her superiors with her competence and foresight. So, on noticing the smudge, on her own initiative she subjected the particular grid in which the smudge appeared to maximum magnification.

The result was far from crystal clear, but intriguing enough for her to take the blowup to her superior, who in turn took it to Aaron Kurtzman.

That afternoon the young woman found herself seated at a console near the front of the room with the "big brains," as she liked to call them.

Thanks to the young go-getter, thirty minutes after Hal Brognola showed up at the War Room, Mack Bolan found himself standing by the landing strip in the northwest quadrant of the Farm.

The soldier's transportation was being wheeled from a nearby corrugated-metal structure that looked just like a typical storage building on a typical farm. Only this building contained the most-sophisticated aviation-servicing equipment known to man. Any jet, any plane, any chopper could be accommodated.

In this instance it was a McDonnell Douglas F-4E Phantom II. Jack Grimaldi was already in the cockpit, going through a preflight instrument check.

Bolan lifted his duffel and slung it over a shoulder. In a few short hours he would be in Los Angeles. From there he would take wing for South America, refueling where necessary until he touched down in Colombia. By the time he got there, Brognola hoped to have more news about the smudge mark, which had turned out to be the minisub.

Apparently the analysts had missed it the first time because they had concentrated on the freighter. Based on the assumption that the ship had to come to a dead stop in order to release the submersible, they had been looking for signs that the *Cartagena* had done so. But every photo, including the infrareds taken at night, showed a clear wake.

Not surprisingly the analysts had concluded that the sub was still on the freighter when it arrived in port. Once they discovered they were wrong, they went back and subjected the wakes in the various photos to a closer computer scrutiny.

At one point, before dawn the last day of her voyage, the *Cartagena* had noticeably slowed. Estimates pegged her at moving from three to five knots. It was then, the analysts now believed, that the minisub had slipped from her secret compartment and sailed southward along the Colombian coast.

The Colombian government didn't like being outfoxed. Brognola's liaison, Colonel Miguel Contillo, had been all for storming the *Cartagena* and taking every last crewman into custody. Contillo was confident he could persuade them to reveal where the sub had gone.

Brognola had talked the officer out of it. El Gato, he'd noted, had gone to great lengths to keep his base of operations a secret. It was unlikely the ship's crew would be privy to such information.

Plus the man had already been put on alert by the incident in the gulf and the Coast Guard attack on the *Parismina*. A raid on his organization in his own country would drive him further underground. He might well close down his whole operation until the heat was off, leaving the authorities high and dry.

Contillo had reluctantly agreed.

"I get the impression he's a bit of a hothead," Brognola had confided to Bolan as they strolled to the north door. "Don't let him box you into a corner down there. If he won't cooperate, bail out. Nailing El Gato isn't worth your life."

"I'll keep that in mind."

BUENAVENTURA, Colombia's leading port, was situated on an island in a bay on the Pacific coast. Thousands of ships reportedly passed in and out every year.

Founded in 1540, the city had many modern buildings, as well as older ones. Scores of its quaint narrow streets were made of cobblestones.

On one of them, tucked into a cul de sac, was a nondescript three-story building painted a dull beige, and it had the distinction of overlooking the stretch of harbor where the *Cartagena* was berthed.

From the outside, a casual passerby would never have guessed that it was anything other than a modest home. Bolan certainly wouldn't have.

As the soldier slid from the brown sedan that had brought him from the airfield, he noticed, though, that the windows were shuttered and that two men in casual clothes lounged near the front door, doing their best to appear inconspicuous. Slight bulges under their jackets told him they were packing heat.

Their clipped hair and spit-shined shoes pegged them as military.

The driver, a young man also in casual clothes who had introduced himself as Captain Alberto Ramirez, hopped out and motioned for Bolan to follow him. "This way, if you please, Señor Belasko." Ramrod stiff, he marched crisply toward the entrance.

There were several soldiers, busy on phones or at computer terminals or studying maps. None showed any interest in the Executioner as he was escorted up a winding staircase to wide double doors. The young officer rapped, and a voice bid them enter in Spanish.

A bulldog of a man with a thick black mustache sat behind a mahogany desk. Setting down a pen, he rose and walked around the desk to greet Bolan. A smile curled his lips, but there was no real warmth to it. "Señor Belasko," he said. "I apologize for not meeting you in person. A man in my position is always so busy...." He let the statement trail off.

"Colonel Contillo," Bolan said. The man's grip was a vise. Bolan matched it and held on for as long as the officer did.

At last Contillo let go. "I see you keep fit. That is good. I was worried that perhaps Señor Brognola had sent a pencil pusher to do a man's job."

Bolan didn't like the officer's attitude or the implication. Taking a seat when bidden, he selected his next words carefully. "Mr. Brognola appreciates how important it is that we stop Estavan Quesada before he can slip through our fingers again."

"Like El Gato did the last time?" Contillo said

stiffly. "I was not in charge then, and I can hardly be blamed for the failure of others. But how noble of Mr. Brognola to condescend to help us poor Colombians. Where would we be without the wonderful guidance of our gringo friends to the north, eh?"

The officer's hostility was as plain as his sneer. Bolan didn't need a degree in psychology to see that Contillo resented American interference in what he judged to be an internal matter. Remembering Brognola's advice, Bolan responded, "I get the message, Colonel. If you don't want me here, have your man drive me back to the airport. I'll take the next flight out."

Contillo blinked. "There is no need to do anything hasty, Mr. Belasko. The president has made it plain that this is to be a joint venture, and I always do as I am ordered. Above all else I am a good soldier."

Bolan didn't doubt it. Whatever else the colonel might be, it was apparent that he ran his operation with commendable precision.

"Please stay," Contillo said. "We are very close to pinpointing El Gato's base of operations. Once we do, you will be in on the kill, as you Americans say."

"You've uncovered a lead?" Bolan asked.

"Maybe. We will know more soon." The colonel spread his fingers on the desk. "For days now my people have been going over the records of every construction company in Buenaventura. Quesada did not build his sub pens out of thin air. Once we find whoever supplied the building materials, we will find him."

The rationale was logical, but flawed. "There's no

guarantee the facility is anywhere near Buenaventura," Bolan said. "and El Gato more than likely relied on middlemen every step of the way to cover his tracks. You could be wasting your time."

Once again the officer took offense. "It is our time to waste, is it not? Unless you have a better idea how we should proceed, I would be grateful if you would keep your criticisms to yourself." Contillo nodded at the captain. "In the meantime you must be tired from your long flight. Ramirez will show you to your room. If you need anything, anything at all, you have but to ask and he will see that it is done."

Bolan was being dismissed. He resented the cavalier treatment, but under the circumstances he did as he was bid and followed the young captain to a third-floor bedroom. Ramirez held the door for him. As he placed his bag on the bed, the Colombian cleared his throat.

"Please accept my apology, Señor Belasko, for the way the colonel just treated you. It is nothing personal, I assure you."

"Oh?" As far as he was concerned, it was yet another example of why he would much rather work alone, even on foreign soil.

"*Sí.* A few years ago a DEA agent from your country accused the colonel of being involved in a drug ring. An investigation proved him innocent of any wrongdoing, but he has never forgiven that agent or your country."

It seemed strange to Bolan that a man who hated Americans would agree to work with one on an operation as sensitive as the Quesada affair. He filed the tidbit for later consideration and asked, "Has there been any activity at the ship?"

"None," Ramirez answered. "We have it under constant watch, but so far there has been no suspicious activity." He started to swing the door shut. "Take your time washing up. In an hour I will return."

Bolan not only washed and changed clothes, but he also rigged a Beretta under his right arm, a Desert Eagle in a holster at the base of his spine, strapped a Solingen throwing knife to his right ankle and stuffed a few covert devices into his pockets. Still in the duffel were an M-16, the P-11 and other odds and ends.

With a little time to kill, Bolan sat in front of the window and scanned the pier. The *Cartagena* wasn't hard to spot. Nor were the three men on an adjacent ship who were loading crates into the hold. They were as clumsy about it as drunken sailors would be, but they weren't drunk. And they weren't seamen. They were more military types in disguise.

It wouldn't take the hardmen on the freighter long to recognize the soldiers for what they were, if they hadn't done so already. The more Bolan saw of the setup, the less he liked it. Small wonder El Gato's men were behaving themselves. They would keep in line until the authorities tired of the surveillance and things could go back to normal.

At the appointed time, Captain Ramirez showed up. He had traded in his white shirt and jacket for a gray suit. "Are you hungry?" he asked.

Bolan wasn't, but he went along for lack of anything better to do. As they descended the stairs, a commotion broke out below.

The captain stopped, his brows knitting. "Excuse me. I must find out what has happened."

Leaning on the banister, Bolan bided his time. In short order Ramirez hastened to rejoin him.

"You have brought us luck, Señor Belasko! A sergeant just told me that we now have a good idea where to find El Gato. In fifteen minutes there will be a staff meeting in the command center downstairs. Your presence is requested."

"I wouldn't miss it," Bolan said, pleased to see action so soon. It was his understanding that once El Gato's lair was located, he would join a strike force that would surround the site to keep the man from escaping. El Gato's nine lives were about to run out.

More than two dozen men and women filled the main room on the ground floor at the appointed time. An excited buzz rippled through them as the eager soldiers awaited word.

Bolan sat in the front row of folding chairs, between Ramirez and a lovely woman with a mane of black hair. He had barely taken his seat when a side door opened and in walked Colonel Contillo. Under the officer's left arm was a manila file.

The room quieted. Contillo nodded at Bolan, then surveyed his staff. He went on at length in Spanish, too quickly for the Executioner to follow, before switching to English. "So for the benefit of our esteemed guest, I will say what must be said in both languages." He paused. "No doubt all of you have heard the news by now. We have a reliable report that Estavan Quesada's base of operations is on the Patia River.''

Bolan heard the woman suck in her breath. He wanted to quiz Ramirez, but the colonel went briskly on.

''Yes, I know. There is no more hellish river in all of South America.'' Contillo spoke for a while in his native tongue, switching to English to say, ''We can thank a handful of Guains for the information. They were among many different Indians forced to work for Quesada as slave labor. Kept under guard, cut off from the outside world, scores died from malnutrition and overwork. Others were gunned down once they had outlived their usefulness.''

Several of the people in the room had Indian lineage. Heated conversations broke out; vows of vengeance were made.

Contillo continued. ''Five Guains managed to escape and make their way to the coast. There they were able to attract a fishing boat that took them to Mosquera, where they reported their ordeal to the police.''

A man wearing the insignia of a major called out, ''When do we leave, Colonel?''

''We should send in a battalion of soldiers!'' someone shouted.

Other voices chimed in, offering suggestions. Contillo raised a hand to restore order, then looked directly at Bolan and said, ''The president has made it clear that we should defer to our American friend in tactical matters. I disagree, but perhaps Señor Belasko would be so kind as to tell us how he thinks we should proceed?"

All eyes swung toward the Executioner.

Bolan disliked being put on the spot. But since he could hardly get up and walk out, and since if he had to do it his way less lives might be lost, he said, "We have a general idea where to find Quesada, not an exact location. I would send in one good man to reconnoiter. Give him enough plastic explosive so that if he finds the sub pens and has the chance, he can do what has to be done without risking anyone else."

Contillo's eyes slitted at the whispers of agreement rippling through the room. "A wise plan, Señor Belasko," he conceded. "But I cannot help thinking that maybe you have an ulterior motive, that perhaps the person you have in mind to go is yourself."

Bolan had tolerated about all he was going to take. "Is there anything wrong with that?"

"No," Contillo said. "I would expect no less from one who comes so highly recommended. But it is impractical. Even, I respectfully submit, extremely naive." He raised his voice. "We all have heard stories about the Patia River. Few men ever go up it alone and come out again. The jungle is thick with jaguars and snakes, and there are Indians a lot less friendly than the Guai tribe."

"That is so," someone said.

"The river itself is treacherous," Contillo went on. "Quicksand and bogs line its banks, and rapids and whirlpools are common the farther one goes." He raked his audience with a hard stare. "One person would not stand a prayer going in there after El Gato. So I propose a compromise."

No one had a word to say this time.

"We will send in a small unit of, say, four people. They will travel by boat up the Patia to see if they can find Quesada's stronghold." Again the colonel focused on Bolan. "I take it that you would like to be one of them?"

"I would."

"Excellent. Then Captain Ramirez, Lieutenant Lazalde and Sergeant Mendoza will go with you. I'll expect all of you in my office to go over the logistics in half an hour. By first light tomorrow, you will be on your way."

The personnel were dismissed. Contillo departed with an orderly in tow.

Ramirez made no attempt to move from his seat, so neither did Bolan. The young officer was clearly troubled. Bolan asked why, and Ramirez seemed to snap out of a daze and answered, "I am fine, *señor*. Really."

Bolan went to rise. If the officer saw fit not to confide in him, he mused, that was Ramirez's business.

"He lies, *americano*."

The soldier twisted.

Next to them stood the striking woman with the luxurious hair. Regarding the captain closely, she elaborated. "It is crazy to send in only four people. Alberto knows that none of us will ever come out of the jungle alive."

"Us?" Bolan said.

The woman offered her slender but firm hand. "Lieutenant Maria Lazalde, at your service. Please excuse me if my accent is not so good. I speak English poorly, I know."

Bolan thought that she was doing fine and remarked as much. "The colonel must have had a reason for picking the two of you. Are you familiar with the terrain along the Patia? Or do you have jungle-combat experience?"

Lazalde's thin right eyebrow lifted. "No one is familiar with the Patia region. It is far to the south, in country inhabited only by a few traders and wild Indians. And worse." She ruefully shook her head. "As for your other question, no, I have never been in a jungle before. I have never even been in combat."

A knot formed in Bolan's gut as he glanced at the captain. "What about you?"

"The same, I am afraid," Ramirez said. "For the life of me, I do not understand why the colonel chose us. There are officers who are much more qualified."

"What about the other soldier he mentioned?" Bolan asked.

"Sergeant Mendoza," Lazalde said. "He has much experience, yes." She laughed oddly. "But I am surprised he was picked. I thought Colonel Contillo liked him. They spend much time together."

Bolan didn't know what to make of the revelations. For all Contillo's faults, the man had impressed him as being model military. There was no reason why he would send a pair of inexperienced officers on the mission they faced. Had Contillo done it out of some sort of perverse revenge for being saddled with him? he wondered.

Lazalde tapped the big man on the shoulder. "Come here, *americano*. I will show you something."

Along the right-hand wall stood a rack containing large maps. The lieutenant spread one out on a table. "Do you see this area?"

It was a map of Colombia. At the bottom, on the southwest coast, jutted a knob of land sixty miles wide, bisected by several winding rivers, one of which was the Patia. The region was lush lowland that received more than three hundred inches of rain a year. To the east it was bordered by the Andes Mountains. Except for two small towns, both on the coast, there were no towns or settlements for hundreds of square miles. El Gato couldn't have selected a more isolated spot if he tried.

Lazalde tapped it. "This is where we are going. The few who have been there say it is hell on earth, worse than the swamps in central Africa. In fact, my people have a nickname for it that tells all there is to know."

Bolan looked at her.

"They call it the Heart of Darkness."

12

The air was hot and muggy. Several hundred yards out to sea, the Executioner leaned on the gunwale of the patrol boat and surveyed the shoreline.

The Colombians hadn't exaggerated. It was a hellhole in there. Tangled growths of lush jungle were broken by rank stretches of steaming swamp. Lieutenant Lazalde had told him that her country's southern Pacific coast was the rainiest spot in all of the Americas, and there was the proof, right before his eyes.

Shifting, Bolan gazed northward but could see no sign of the destroyer that had brought them from Buenaventura to within a few miles of their goal. On board was Colonel Contillo and a special army contingent of 150 soldiers.

The patrol boat glided sleek and low in the water, its powerful engine rumbling. The hull reminded Bolan of a Mako powerboat, only longer. It was painted in shades of camouflage green. Thanks to a turbocharged power plant that could generate more than four hundred horses, it could do close to sixty knots.

At the moment they were barely doing twenty. Captain Ramirez was at the wheel, his eyes focused on a broad gap in the verdant growth to the south. "The Patia River," he announced somberly.

The moment of truth was almost upon them. Bolan took stock of his companions as he locked and loaded his M-16. All three wore fatigues, different from his only in that they were Colombian military issue and not U.S. made. All three were armed with Madsen M-1953 submachine guns, standard issue for many South American armed forces. In side holsters they carried a version of the Colt 1911 A-1 pistol. They also had sheath knives.

Of the three, Ramirez was the only one with a bad case of nerves. Lazalde seemed to have a knack for taking everything in stride. Her expression was grim, but there was no doubt she had herself completely under control. Bolan knew he could depend on her in a pinch.

The sergeant was another matter. Mendoza was an unknown factor. A husky, brooding man, he hadn't said ten words to the Executioner since they met. The noncom kept to himself, speaking to the officers only when addressed. He appeared to be one tough customer, but Bolan had learned long ago how deceiving appearances could be.

The strident cry of a bird rent the gloomy jungle as the patrol boat drew near to the river's mouth. Ramirez started, then caught himself and nervously licked his lips. Mendoza, Bolan noticed, made no attempt to hide his disgust.

The boat nosed into the Patia. It rode so low that Bolan could have reached down and dipped a hand in the murky water. Mounted at the stern was a pair of depth charges. To the right of the control console, attached to a high tripod bolted to the deck, was a Browning M-2 heavy machine gun. Mendoza stood ready to use it at all times.

Given all the talk about rapids and whirlpools, Bolan had imagined the Patia River would be a raging torrent. Instead, he found himself cruising up the middle of a sluggish belt of brown water that gave the illusion of being thick enough for a person to walk on.

"We are being sized up for dinner," Lazalde said, and pointed.

Near the north shore a large, blunt snout and a pair of eyes had broken the surface. The eyes regarded the boat and its passengers with cold menace.

"A caiman," Bolan said.

"They infest this region," Lazalde revealed. "As do anacondas, boas, coral snakes and poisonous frogs and toads."

"Something was mentioned about unfriendly Indians back in Buenaventura."

Lazalde pursed her lips and nodded at the verdant jungle. "No one knows how many tribes live back in there. Most keep to themselves. They shun our kind as if we carry the plague." She paused. "A few years ago, seven missionaries flew deep into the interior. It was in all the newspapers, how they were going to convert the savages."

"What happened?"

"What else. A supply plane went in and found all seven had been butchered." Lazalde adjusted her cap so the brim shielded her eyes from the burning sun.

"There are some things in this world better left alone."

The patrol boat rounded a bend. Immediately the river narrowed until it was no more than fifty feet across. Ramirez throttled back and put the gear in neutral. Opening a cubbyhole on the console, he took out a coiled plumb. "Sergeant Mendoza, if you would do the honors," he said in Spanish.

Without saying a word, the noncom took it and stepped to the port side. Dipping the lead weight into the water, he let the line unravel until the weight hit the bottom. "Three meters," he announced.

Bolan was surprised, and he could tell he wasn't the only one. The river was scarcely deep enough for a minisub to fully submerge. It made no sense for El Gato to choose a waterway where his submersibles would be exposed as they traveled back and forth from the sea. Then again, Bolan had to remind himself that the Patia River was so remote, no one would ever spot them.

The captain pushed on at a cautious crawl. Birds squawked, whistled and cawed on both sides of the river. Huge butterflies flitted around brilliant flowers.

Every now and then Bolan saw the water ripple, as if to the passage of unseen creatures. Caimans became more numerous, many sunning themselves on gravel bars and mud banks. Mingled with them were small birds that walked around and over the reptiles with impunity.

The Executioner glimpsed movement in the trees to the south. Spindly gray monkeys were scampering about, some hanging from prehensile tails high above the forest floor. On spying the boat, many swung to branches nearer the river for a better look.

"Spider monkeys," Lazalde said, and held up her left hand to show a tiny scar on her second knuckle. "When I was a little girl, my mother took me to the zoo, and I tried to feed peanuts to one. It bit me."

Bolan peered inland. Due to the twists and turns in the river, it was impossible to see more than a few hundred feet ahead. The prospect of an ambush was very real. He flicked the selector lever on his rifle to autofire.

The humidity had to be close to one hundred percent. Combined with a temperature at or above the one hundred mark, it made for sweltering, moist heat that drenched Bolan as if he were in a sauna.

Beads of sweat dotted Ramirez's brow. Often he nervously licked his lips. It was evident that he would rather be anywhere than where he was. The man would bear watching should they engage enemy forces.

Mendoza acted bored by the whole business. He was alert enough, but in a relaxed manner, a contradiction only a professional soldier could truly understand and appreciate. When, on occasion, his gaze drifted past Bolan, there was no hint of friendliness in his expression.

The Pacific was half a mile behind them when yet another bend appeared. The river narrowed to less than fifteen feet, widening again beyond. Angled across the narrow point was a wide tree, the trunk no more than ten feet above the water. Ramirez started to ease the patrol boat underneath when Lazalde suddenly sprang forward, grabbed his arm and barked, "Be careful! Look there!"

Bolan had been scouring the north bank. Turning, he saw the reason for her alarm coiled around the tree.

"Anaconda!" Mendoza grated.

It had to be more than twenty feet long and a foot wide in the center. Yellowish scales on the bottom blended to dark brown above and were dappled with large black circles. The huge triangular head lay draped over one thick coil. Its eyes were open, yet it wheezed softly as if snoring. A prominent bulge testified to the fact it had eaten recently and was sleeping off the meal.

As Bolan looked on, the bulge moved deeper into the anaconda's digestive tract, the snake's smooth hide rippling and swelling.

"No one do anything," Lazalde cautioned. "I have heard that if you do not bother them, most of the time they will not bother you."

Ramirez was as rigid as a board. Swallowing hard, he permitted the patrol boat to coast under the tree. Since there was no room to pass by on either side, they had to float directly underneath the giant beast.

The bow passed the tree without incident, then the captain and the lieutenant, both stiff with fear. Sergeant Mendoza showed no reaction.

It was Bolan's turn next. Just as he drifted below the snake, it lifted its head and looked right at him. The soldier didn't take his eyes off the reptile until the trunk was safely behind them.

"¡Madre di Dios!" Ramirez exclaimed, and

crossed himself. "I never want to see another one of those things as long as I live!"

The officer spoke too soon. Hardly were the words out of his mouth than Bolan spied another giant specimen on a log at the river's edge, basking. It paid them no heed. The soldier had read somewhere that anacondas often traveled in pairs. Indians claimed that if one was attacked, its mate would speed to its rescue.

Ramirez gave the log as wide a berth as the river allowed. Another turn put them well out of danger, and he increased speed to ten knots, as fast as they dared go given the river conditions.

Over forty minutes dragged by. The river width varied from fifteen to thirty feet, on average. Birds with bright plumage were everywhere, as were various kinds of monkeys. Once howlers screamed at them, rocking the jungle with booming cries.

The captain had the sergeant check the depth from time to time. It varied by no more than a foot at any given point, averaging nine feet overall.

By noon they had been on the river for four hours and seen no sign of human habitation, no trace of any sub pens. Ramirez mopped his forehead and said, "I begin to have serious doubts, Señor Belasko. This might be—how would you say it?—a wild horse's chase."

"Close enough," Bolan said. "But we keep going until we know for sure."

"Is anyone else as thirsty as I am?" Lazalde asked, stepping to a cooler she had brought along.

Bolan was going to accept a bottle of water. Unexpectedly gunfire cracked to the east. The captain promptly slowed. Mendoza moved to the Browning. They all listened as the shots tapered, then erupted again seconds later, coming closer.

"What does it mean?" Lazalde asked.

Just then Bolan noticed a break in the vegetation to the south where a tributary fed into the Patia River. Plants hemmed it in on either side, and tree branches formed a canopy above. Prodding Ramirez on the elbow, Bolan nodded at the opening and said, "It would be best if we took cover until we know what's going on."

"I agree." Without delay the captain angled the patrol boat over. The stream was so narrow that there were only a few inches to spare as Ramirez skillfully backed the craft in and killed the engine.

Bolan pulled limbs lower to screen the windshield. The others took his cue and did what they could to add to the camouflage.

Meanwhile the shooting stopped. Another flurry of shots broke out a minute later, louder than ever. Gruff laughter reached their ears.

Bolan crouched next to the gunwale, aft of the cabin. Around them the jungle had gone totally silent. Not so much as a bird stirred anywhere.

The throb of a propeller heralded the approach of another vessel. It was nearly abreast of the stream before it came into sight. Cruising brazenly down the middle of the river was a minisubmarine, the conning tower and most of the afterdeck above water. Two men occupied the tower while a third stood on the afterdeck with a high-powered rifle in hand.

"El Gato's men!" Lazalde whispered.

The man with the rifle intently scanned the south shore. He swiveled toward the creek and might have spotted the patrol boat in another instant had not one of the men in the conning tower called out and pointed to the north.

Bolan saw several marmosets watching the sub go by. They were cute little monkeys with tufts of white hair rimming their ears and long striped tails. The head of one exploded as the man on the afterdeck cored its brain with a well-placed shot. Before the other two could flee, the gunner dropped them both with swift, accurate shots. Then the man laughed.

In moments the submarine had sailed past and vanished around the last bend.

Lazalde's face acquired a flinty cast. "Those bastards!" she said "To kill such innocent creatures for sport!"

"With any luck the anaconda will drop on one of them," Ramirez commented.

"How I wish," Lazalde said.

Ramirez waited a full five minutes before he cranked the engine and edged out into the Patia again. More gun shots came from the west, growing fainter. The captain turned the patrol boat upriver. "At least now we know this is not a horse chase," he commented.

Bolan was thinking about the minisub. There had been no way to determine if it was the same one that had been on the *Cartagena*. The one he had seen in the Gulf of Mexico and the one wrecked in California had been identical, ·as near as he could tell, so it was likely that all the subs in El Gato's growing fleet looked exactly the same. None, for obvious reasons, had identifying numbers or letters.

The Colombians were more alert from then on. Mendoza never took his hands off the machine gun, Lazalde held her Madsen at the ready and Ramirez, oddly enough, shook off his case of bad nerves and lived up to the training the Colombian army had invested in him.

The boat navigated inland another mile and a half. A spine of rocky land blocked their view of the next stretch of river, and Bolan rose on his toes to see if he could catch a glimpse of whatever lay ahead. He couldn't. Placing a foot on a seat, he was straightening when the craft purred around the point and into a living nightmare.

Lazalde stifled a cry and recoiled, leveling her subgun. Mendoza turned to the right and left as if unsure in which direction he should cut loose. Only Ramirez made no move to employ a weapon, but his hands gripped the wheel so hard, his knuckles were pale.

It was understandable.

The river was choked with caimans. From bank to bank, for half the length of a football field, alligators of all sizes crammed the water. The captain had no opportunity to turn aside or throw the boat into reverse. All he could do was reduce speed to a snail's pace as the vessel slid in among the armored terrors.

"God help us!" Lazalde breathed.

Bolan shared her sentiments. Caimans scraped against the hull on both sides and closed in around the stern. The boat sat so low in the water that many of the brutes were an arm's length away, if that. Jaws snapped; tails slapped. A few of the larger bulls made aborted rushes but didn't try to come up over the side. Yet.

"How the hell did that sub get through?" Lazalde snapped.

Bolan stabbed a finger at a bullet-riddled body lying upside down in darkly stained water. "There's your answer." Other dead caimans were scattered among the living, some being feasted on by their fellows.

"I can do the same, Captain," Mendoza proposed, swiveling the Browning.

"And run the chance of having El Gato's people hear?" Ramirez said. "No. We will try to get through without shooting any."

Bolan was nearest a gunwale. He made no sudden moves in the belief that if he stood stock-still, the caimans wouldn't be incited to attack. But he was mistaken.

Bellowing like an enraged hippo, an eight-footer lunged, scrambling up onto the spiny backs of those in front of it to get at the boat. Its front legs hooked on the gunwale and it levered toward the Executioner, its massive jaws yawning wide to enclose him in their iron grip. Bolan threw himself backward.

The caiman hadn't gained enough momentum to carry it all the way up and over the side. Tail thrashing wildly, it teetered like a grotesque seesaw. Gravity took over and down it went, landing amid other caimans that bit at it in annoyance. The bull turned on them in unbridled fury. In a flash a battle royal broke out, with smaller caimans scattering before the bull's onslaught.

The roiling, seething mass threatened to spill onto the boat. Bolan grabbed the captain and ordered, "Get us out of here! Full throttle!"

Ramirez hesitated, but only until a five-foot gator clawed onto the gunwale and would have dropped onto the deck if not for Lazalde, who rushed in close and kicked it in the shoulder, tumbling the reptile into the river. Throwing the engine wide open, the captain plowed into the caimans ahead, scattering them. Those not struck were incited to flee by those seeking to get out of the way.

It seemed as if the boat would reach clear water without mishap. Then a big caiman somehow gained a purchase on the stern and hauled itself up beside one of the depth charges. Dark eyes twinkling, it began to slide toward its prey.

Bolan resorted to the Beretta, smoothly unleathering the 9 mm pistol. The suppressor coughed twice, twin holes blossoming high on the caiman's head.

The soldier had gone for the brain, but apparently he had missed because the alligator kept on coming, its claws clacking on the deck, its tail sweeping violently back and forth. The Executioner took precise aim at a spot midway between its eyes and an inch or so above them. His next round drilled the spot cleanly.

The caiman gave a convulsive shudder. Mouth agape, it slid to a lifeless halt at the feet of Lazalde. She let breath escape her lips and glanced at him. "Thank you, *señor*. I am in your debt."

Ramirez whooped as the patrol boat raced into the open. He hadn't observed their close call. Turning, he almost tripped over the caiman, and blanched. "Throw it overboard, Sergeant. I don't want it stinking up our boat."

Before Mendoza could comply, Lazalde craned her neck and asked, "Is that a lake ahead?"

Bolan recalled no reference to a lake on the map he had studied, yet the Patia River widened drastically to form just that. "Slow down," he advised. To the north the water was bordered by swampland. Clusters of trees and high reeds offered plenty of places to hide. "Get us under cover over there."

Ramirez did as he was told, his features reflecting his puzzlement. Once the boat idled in deep shadows, he queried, "Why do we halt, Señor Belasko, when we might be close to El Gato's lair?"

"We're a lot closer than you think," Bolan said, nodding at four gleaming shapes far out on the water. The quartet sailed from north to south, executed a ninety-degree turn and headed westward.

"They are minisubs!" Lazalde declared.

Helping himself to a pair of binoculars on the console, Bolan adjusted the central focusing control. The subs were drilling in formation. One was slightly in front of the others, and the rest were keying their maneuvers off it. He told the soldiers.

"You mean to say that El Gato conducts a training school for those who operate his submarines?" Ramirez said in amazement.

It made perfect sense, Bolan reflected. The drug lord could hardly advertise for sub drivers in the classifieds. Quesada probably employed one or two experts who trained those who heard of the positions through criminal contacts.

The Executioner roved the binoculars around the perimeter of the lake. More jungle flanked the water to the east, while a cliff pockmarked with caves reared skyward to the south. At water level was the biggest of them all. Within it was a hint of movement. "Bingo," he said under his breath.

"Señor!" Lazalde said urgently, poking his shoulder with her subgun.

Bolan gazed out over the water. He didn't need the binoculars to see that the four minisubs had changed direction, and that their new heading was taking them straight toward the patrol boat.

"They must have seen us!" Ramirez said. "So be it." He reached for the throttle. "We will die as soldiers should!"

13

The Executioner had seen the same thing time and again. It was always the ones with limited combat experience who were all too eager to indulge in mindless heroics. Shouldering the young officer aside, he turned off the engine, saying, "There's no need for any of us to die just yet. I don't think they know we're here."

Moments later the Executioner was proved correct when the four subs made another tight turn and headed toward the towering cliff.

Ramirez hung his head. "I am most sorry, Señor Belasko. In my excitement I forgot that Colonel Contillo told us not to do anything without your okay. Please forgive me."

"No harm done," Bolan said, and let the matter drop. Through the binoculars he watched the quartet of subs sail into the cavern at the base of the cliff. No sooner were they out of sight than something unfurled from above to cover the cavern entrance. Whatever it was, it had been painted to match the color of the cliff face and blended in perfectly. No one would ever suspect the cavern was there.

"What is our next step?" Lazalde inquired.

"We wait until dark," Bolan informed her, "then we go in closer to investigate."

Ramirez fidgeted. "Excuse me for saying this, sir. Would it not be wiser to immediately head for the destroyer so we can report to the colonel? He will call in an air strike, and by tomorrow night El Gato and his sub pens will be, as you Americans say, history."

"It wouldn't be the smart thing to do just now." He indicated the sun, which was well on its downward arc. "Not unless you want to run into that sub patrolling the river in the dark."

Sergeant Mendoza finally had a comment to make. In Spanish, he said, "That is not your real reason, is it?"

"No," Bolan admitted. "I meant what I said about doing this with as little loss of life as possible. We have enough explosives on board to destroy the cavern ourselves. I intend to go in there and see if it's feasible."

Neither Mendoza nor Ramirez liked the plan, but they held their tongues. Only the lieutenant accepted it without making a sour face. Turning to the dead caiman, she said, "What about this thing? Shouldn't we throw it overboard?"

The Executioner shook his head. Drawing his Ka-bar knife, he knelt beside the caiman. "Some of you give me a hand."

"What are you doing?" Ramirez asked.

"You'll see."

It was hard, messy work. First they had to roll the heavy caiman onto its back, then they had to slit it from chin to tail. A nauseating stench rose as the gator's insides oozed out. One by one the organs had to be sliced free of the body and tossed overboard.

Lazalde wrapped her arms around a steaming mass of intestines. As she started to lift them, her foot slipped on the caiman's liver and she fell hard onto her backside. The intestines spilled across her chest and stomach, covering her face and most of her hair. Violently she cast the intestines off, pushed to her knees and doubled over, retching.

Bolan helped her to stand, then guided her to the gunwale. She mumbled thanks as she bent low over the reeds and finished emptying her stomach. When she was done, she wiped her mouth with the back of her sleeve and glanced up at him.

"You must think me awfully weak."

"Not at all," Bolan assured her, and grinned. "Most people who swallow raw alligator guts do the same thing."

Lazalde grinned back. "Known many caiman eaters, have you?" She splashed water onto her face and hair and went back to work.

Once the caiman's insides had been disposed of, Lazalde and Mendoza sloshed the deck as clean as they could make it. While they were occupied, Bolan worked on the caiman's hide with his knife. He cut a narrow slit between the eyes and two circular patches from the skin that hung down under the lower jaw so the caiman's head would fit over his own.

Ramirez caught on. "You cannot be thinking what I think you are thinking."

"Haven't you ever heard of the Trojan horse?" Bolan countered.

The next step was to prepare the plastic explosives, along with enough detonator cord to suit Bolan, and several detonators. The plastique was already wrapped in waterproof plastic. Bolan rummaged around the patrol boat and came up with a toolbox used for minor repairs. In it was a roll of duct tape, which he wrapped around the det cord and electronic detonators to keep them from getting wet.

The Colombians had wondered why he insisted on leaving the caiman's legs intact. He had directed that they remove the bones and scoop out the flesh, but not sever the skin. His motive became apparent when he stuffed the packets of explosive into the legs and added tape to ensure they wouldn't slip out. The det cord and the detonators went under his shirt.

Ramirez ran a hand over the caiman. "You are a most devious man, *señor*. I am glad you are not El Gato, or we would be dead by now."

The rest of the afternoon passed quietly. They ate from the cooler Lazalde had brought. "It was either my own food, or army rations," she joked at one point. "And they taste worse than caiman guts."

Sunset transformed the Patia from a dusky brown to blazing red.

"It looks like a river of blood, doesn't it?" Ramirez remarked.

Twilight claimed the jungle. Still Bolan didn't give the order to move out. He was leaving nothing to chance. They would get only one try, and if they blew it, their lives were forfeit.

The vault of sky over the tropics darkened, giving birth to myriad stars.

No lights shone anywhere on the river, nor were any visible in the vicinity of the cliff.

Bolan handed one of the short oars kept on board for emergency use to Mendoza and said, "We'll paddle in shifts, fifteen minutes at a time. Us first, then the two officers."

No one argued. They knew why, and they knew what was at stake.

Sinking onto his knee next to the starboard gunwale, Bolan dipped the oar into the water and shoved off. At first the boat responded sluggishly and was difficult to propel. But as they gained speed, it knifed the surface cleanly, swinging to the south and paralleling the shoreline. Other than the slight splash of the oars and an occasional creak of the hull, they made no noise that would give them away.

The night was filled with sounds, though. Caimans bellowed, frogs croaked, insects chirped and buzzed, birds shrieked. Inland, now and again, jaguars roared. And once a hideous, wavering cry carried on the wind, a cry unlike any Bolan had ever heard.

By the Executioner's figuring they were halfway to the cliff when the air throbbed faintly, as if to the beat of an invisible drum.

Lazalde cocked her head. "What is that?"

"I do not hear anything," Mendoza said.

Bolan knew better. He happened to be paddling at the time, and he promptly made for the shore. "Get under cover, fast."

The sound was as familiar as Bolan's own heartbeat, and well it should be, since he had heard it countless times. He stroked furiously, the rhythmic sounds of rotors growing louder by the second.

Just as the patrol boat glided under the overhanging limbs of a gigantic tree perched on the bank, a wide beam of light speared the night, playing over the water. A helicopter swooped in low, its silhouette an inky outline against the backdrop of starry heavens.

Bolan and the soldiers ducked. He noted that the chopper was small and fitted with pontoons. It looped toward the cliff, losing altitude rapidly. At the same time, the covering over the cavern entrance rolled upward, evidently winched by unseen machinery. Light spilled from within.

Like a homing pigeon returning to its roost, the helicopter flew into the cavern and was gone. Once again the cover descended, blocking off the light. Darkness reclaimed the Patia, and the wild things resumed their nightly refrain.

"El Gato has a visitor," Ramirez deduced.

"Or maybe it is El Gato himself," Lazalde said.

Bolan didn't go on until he was certain no more choppers were due to arrive. Nodding at Mendoza, he bent into a stroke. The patrol boat moved out from under the tree, but not far. The Executioner preferred to stay close to land.

A finger of weed-choked land poked into the Patia approximately two dozen yards to the west of the cliff. Bolan took the boat behind it and swung broadside. Setting down the oar, he slid the hide of the slain gator close to the side.

"What you attempt is madness, *señor*," Ramirez said. "This is a job for the Colombian air force, not you."

Lazalde put a hand on the Executioner's shoulder. "Listen to him. It is not too late to change your mind."

Bolan sat to strip off his combat boots and socks. "What if you're right about Quesada being on that chopper? What if he leaves before the fighters can get here? We owe it to all those whose lives El Gato has ruined to put a stop to his scheme here and now."

"I can see your point," Lazalde said, "but I still think you put too great a burden on yourself. Quesada is a Colombian. He is our problem." She sighed. "You take his evil much too personally."

"That's just the point," Bolan countered. "Evil is supposed to be taken personally. If more people did, if they fought back instead of turned their backs on it, our world would be a much better place in which to live."

Mendoza snorted. "Are all *americanos* such dreamers?"

Paying the noncom no heed, Bolan leaned the M-16 against a seat. From a backpack he had brought along, he pulled out the P-11 ZUB and strapped its special holster around his waist. The Dolphina breathing apparatus went into a pants pocket.

Next Bolan carefully eased over the side, alert for movement nearby. Treading water, he tried not to think of what would happen should a caiman come up on him from below. There would be no warning.

Its iron jaws would clamp on him, and he would be pulled under before the others could lift a finger. "Pass me the hide," he said.

It took Lazalde and Ramirez both to lift it and align the skin over Bolan so that the head of the caiman fitted over his own. To his relief, the stiff hide had enough buoyancy to float without any great effort on his part. He could see out through the mouth and the slit he had cut. The reek of dry blood and gore was atrocious.

"Take care," Lazalde said.

"Stay put until I get back," Bolan directed, his voice hollow and muffled. Pushing off, he swam toward the base of the cliff. The night was pitch-black. He could distinguish the bulbous tip of the caiman's nose but not much beyond it.

The water was warmer than Bolan had anticipated. He covered a third of the distance when suddenly bubbles stirred the surface in front of him, and a long shape rose straight up out of the depths.

Bolan stopped dead inches from a caiman twice the size of the one he had killed. It dwarfed him, a primeval dragon that could cut him in two with a single bite. He slipped a hand onto the hilt of the Ka-bar knife and braced for its onslaught, but it merely stared with unblinking eyes, a few lazy swishes of the end of its tail the only sign that it was alive.

The Executioner waited for the caiman to make the first move. He went limp so he could float without treading water, since any motion might spur it into rushing him.

Bolan figured that the mix of his scent and the hide's had the alligator confused. It couldn't make up its mind whether he was prey or a fellow predator. Reaching back, he gripped the tail trailing behind him and imitated the caiman's own movements.

The beast uttered a grunt, prompting Bolan to draw his knife half out of its sheath. If the creature came at him, he would drop down under it and try to slash open its stomach. The belly was its Achilles' heel, the only place where a blade could inflict crippling harm.

Awful moments dragged by. Bolan wondered if the caiman was going to stay there all night. As if in answer, it grunted once more and sank straight down, disappearing in an agitated froth. Something brushed Bolan's left foot.

Bolan got out of there while he could. Using a breast stroke, he reached the cliff in safety and paused. He raised the hide high enough to scan the jagged rock face. Then, keeping his back to the cliff in the event he was attacked, he swam slowly toward the cavern.

At first Bolan couldn't pinpoint whatever was used to cover the opening. Groping the rough, pockmarked surface, he poked and prodded until his hands made contact with something that gave way under pressure. Exercising care not to disturb it, he roamed his fingertips in ever widening circles until he found a thick edge. Prying revealed that the camouflage cover was made of heavy canvas.

The soldier adjusted the caiman's hide, pulled the canvas far enough out for him to slip inside and slowly swam into El Gato's lair. He hugged the wall where the shadows were deepest. Before him unfolded a marvel of ingenuity that boggled the imagination.

The cavern was immense. High overhead jagged stalactites hung in untidy phalanxes. The ceiling formed a dome, while the sides were sheer and smooth.

It was the whirl of activity in the center of the cavern that intrigued Bolan the most. He counted twelve sub pens, only three of which were unoccupied. Four of the other nine were under construction, work crews bustling around them like drone bees repairing a hive.

The pens fronted five corrugated-metal buildings of varying size. Two were huge hangarlike affairs where, Bolan suspected, the initial work on the subs was performed. Another building appeared to be an office. Yet another was long and low, as a barracks would be.

Heavy machinery was everywhere. Crates were stacked high at several points. Behind one such stack was the chopper, the rotor head and the blades the only parts visible.

All of the twenty to thirty men that Bolan could see were engrossed in the jobs they were doing. No one was watching the entrance. He felt confident in swimming nearer.

As Bolan was focused on the enemy, he didn't look closely at a knob of rock he passed. One of the caiman's legs snagged on it. Drawn up short, he twisted and dipped into the water to peer up under the hide. It was then that he realized the rock was no rock at all but instead a cleverly disguised photoelectric cell. He had broken the invisible beam.

A metallic rumble echoed in the cavern. A small motorboat manned by two gunners, one holding an AK-47, swept from around the sub pens. They arrowed toward Bolan, the outboard roaring. A small spotlight flared to life and skimmed across the surface of the water.

Bolan thought fast. Yanking out the Dolphina, he inserted the mouthpiece and turned the control knob. Remembering to breathe slowly, he tucked at the waist, then dived, going deep. In his ears thrummed the growl of the outboard's prop.

Twenty feet down, Bolan stopped and looked up. The water distorted the image of the motorboat, but he saw the shooter with the AK-47 lean out and open fire. Rounds stitched the hide, making it jerk and jump as a real caiman would. In seconds it began to sink, the legs spread, the tail hanging as limp as a wet towel.

The firing stopped. Satisfied they had done their job, the gunners circled back toward the dock.

Bolan rose to intercept the hide before it sank from sight. Underwater it seemed to weigh five times as much as it had up above. He had to hold it with both arms as he kicked to propel himself toward the rear of the cavern.

The last sub pen in the row lay forty feet from the west wall. Bolan rose until his eyes were above the surface and checked whether anyone was in the immediate area. The pen appeared to be deserted.

Adopting a side stroke, he swam to it and reached for a handhold so he could pull himself out of the water.

At that moment, a hatch clanged open on top of the sub and a bald head popped out. Bolan instantly submerged several feet. Afraid he had not been quick enough, he drew the P-11.

A face appeared on top of the pen wall. It was the man from the sub. He acted more curious than alarmed, as if he weren't quite sure he had seen something. Leaning down, he scrutinized the depths and spied Bolan.

The Executioner aimed and fired. The pistol made no more noise than a BB gun and had little recoil.

At that range the dart bored into the smuggler's forehead with the force of a bullet. As the man's head snapped back, he grabbed at his brow, stiffened and slid over the wall.

Swiftly Bolan rose to catch the body before it made a loud splash. He only partly succeeded. Flattening against the pen, he listened for an outcry. There was none.

The Executioner had to dispose of the corpse before he could get on with what had to be done. Swimming to a flat stone shelf beside the pen, he clambered out of the water, then hauled the hide and the body up next to him so the former wouldn't sink and the latter wouldn't float off.

Fingers flying, Bolan removed the packets of explosive from the caiman's legs and placed them aside. Pushing the dead man back into the water, he shoved both flapping forearms into the smuggler's pants. His next step was to take off the man's belt and lash the ankles securely.

The body bobbed gently. Left unattended, it would drift into the open.

Bolan lifted the hide. It fit over the man as snugly as a glove. He had to bend the bottom edge to conceal the figure's shirt. Placing his feet flat against the mock caiman, he thrust it away from the shelf so the current could take hold.

There was no time to spare. Bolan gathered up the plastic explosives and climbed to the top of the sub pen. A catwalk led past a wall of crates. He hurried in among them without being seen and squatted to await the result of his diversion. It was not long in coming.

"Hey, Stenson!" someone hollered. "You missed one! There's another damn gator out there!"

"Are you sure? We didn't see any others!" Stenson replied.

"Harvey isn't lying!" someone else interjected. "I can see it, too. Get the hell over here before the stinking thing tries to eat one of us!"

The outboard snarled into gear. A gap in the crates allowed Bolan to see the motorboat putter around the far end of the pens.

Bolan glanced at the decoy. It was thirty feet out and drifting toward the entrance. Some of the workers had stopped what they were doing to watch the gator killer close in.

Stenson wore a scowl of annoyance. He sighted down the autorifle, tracked the bogus caiman several seconds and opened fire. A cheer went up from the workers as a 7.62 mm hailstorm ripped into the target.

Counting on the drug lord's underlings to be distracted long enough for him to reach different cover, Bolan headed for the buildings. He rounded a cluster of oil drums, skirted a fuel pump and darted in between a large metal trash bin and a parked forklift.

By then the hide and the body under it had been riddled. The holes notwithstanding, the "caiman" refused to sink. Stenson's scowl deepened. He produced a hand grenade from a jacket pocket and said something to the man handling the outboard. The motorboat swung wide to return to the dock. As it did, Stenson yanked the pin and heaved the bomb.

Another resounding cheer greeted the deafening explosion that obliterated every trace of the gator skin and the dead man.

The blast had two unforeseen effects. First, Bolan saw thick clouds of dust and bits of stone rain from the roof of the cavern. The workers didn't seem to be fazed, but he found it highly interesting.

Then something else took place that was even more riveting. A door in one of the large buildings opened, and out strolled two people.

One of them was Colonel Miguel Contillo.

14

Mack Bolan didn't feel the least bit surprised. But then, the chopper that had arrived earlier, the small one with the pontoons and spotlight, had been exactly like the one Colonel Contillo had insisted on bringing from Buenaventura, lashed to the foredeck of the destroyer. For aerial reconnaissance, the colonel had said.

The other man was tall and whipcord lean and dressed in a well-cut suit. A gold earring adorned an ear, and gold rings encircled every finger. In his left hand a thin cigarillo jutted from a gold cigarette holder. In Spanish he called out in an imperious tone, "Tejo! What was that explosion?"

A man standing beside a sub spun around. "Boss! It was nothing. Just the American killing another of those filthy beasts with a grenade."

The workers went on about their business as Stenson and the motorboat headed for the end of the pens.

Bolan studied the tall man. So that was Estavan Quesada, El Gato, the criminal genius whose coffers were fed by the suffering of untold others. Each ounce of gold the man wore had been paid for by the ruined lives of countless addicts. Bolan intended to make sure that the man paid for every one.

A radio clipped to Contillo's belt crackled. He held it to his mouth and spoke a few words that Bolan didn't quite catch. Someone responded, and Contillo grinned. "They come, Estavan."

Quesada smiled, took a puff on his cigarette and called out, "Tejo! Raise the canvas! We have guests coming!"

Men scrambled to obey. A generator purred to life, machinery whined and across the cavern, the bottom of the heavy canvas hiked slowly upward.

Bolan took advantage of the lull to take the det cord and detonators from under his shirt and unwrap them. While everyone was watching the entrance, he stealthily retraced his steps to the fuel pump and placed a charge beside it. He also placed one behind the oil drums. Crates stenciled Torpedoes and Ammunition rated similar treatment. Unwinding the det cord, the soldier crept back to his hiding place and linked the charges to a pair of detonators. He didn't set the timers yet. He wanted to see who the new arrivals were.

The canvas was more than halfway up. A boat engine rumbled, and into the lair glided a craft all too familiar to Bolan. It was the patrol boat, and Sergeant Mendoza had the wheel. There was no sign of Captain Ramirez or Lieutenant Lazalde.

The noncom didn't act in any way upset at being among his sworn enemies. In fact, he waved to Tejo and exchanged comments as the boat neared an empty dock and slipped neatly into the berth. Tejo barked orders. A pair of gunners jumped onto the boat, bent and roughly hauled Ramirez and Lazalde to their feet.

Both officers had their wrists bound behind their backs. Blood trickled from a nasty gash on the captain's temple, and the lieutenant had a darkening bruise on her jaw. They glared at Mendoza as the sergeant led the way up a metal walk to where the colonel and Quesada waited.

"Well done, Sergeant," Contillo said as the noncom saluted. "I knew that I could rely on you."

Ramirez bristled. "Colonel, what is the meaning of this outrage? First he attacks us, and now here you are, with this pig!" Ramirez tossed his head in contempt at Quesada.

El Gato had been about to take another puff on his cigarette. A sinister smirk creased his mouth. He transferred the cigarette holder to his left hand, stepped up to the young officer and laid a hand on Ramirez's shoulder. "No intelligent animal ever seeks its own extinction," he said so quietly that Bolan barely heard the words. Then his right hand flashed. A blade gleamed in the glow of a floodlight mounted on the building.

Ramirez cried out as his abdomen was sliced open from hip to hip. His intestines started to slide out, and he doubled over in a vain bid to stem the fatal flow. "You—" he sputtered at his killer, but couldn't finish the statement. Weakening rapidly, he sank to his knees.

Contillo sighed. "You always were a jackass, Ramirez. That is why I picked you for this mission. I did not want someone who would give us any trouble."

He glanced at Lazalde. "How about you, Lieutenant? Anything you would like to say?"

Lazalde's features were hard with hatred. "Only that I regret not being able to report you to the president."

Contillo chuckled. "Ah, yes. That idiot. Unfortunately for you, my dear, I have fooled him completely. I am one of his most trusted advisers."

The lieutenant puckered her mouth as if she were going to spit on him. "A few years ago, when that American agent accused you of being involved in drugs, it was true, wasn't it?"

"Of course," Contillo admitted. "I have been on Estavan's payroll for a long time. But I am always able to cover my tracks."

At that moment Ramirez uttered a low groan and keeled forward until his forehead rested on the ground. Tears streamed from the corners of his eyes. With a monumental effort, he rasped, "I pray that you pay for your crimes, bastard!"

"Who will make me? You?" Contillo taunted. A thought seemed to strike him and he swung toward Mendoza. "Wait a minute. Where is the American?"

The noncom was standing at attention. "Wasn't he killed? I heard shooting and an explosion, so I assumed that he had been disposed of."

"That was a caiman," Contillo said.

"But he was disguised as one," Mendoza revealed, and briefly explained.

Contillo visibly relaxed. "Clever of him. Very

clever. But he has been blown to pieces, so we need not worry. I will contact his superior and report that he was killed by savage Indians on his way into the interior."

Lazalde couldn't take her eyes off Ramirez, who wheezed noisily, his chest straining for every breath. "Is that what you will tell the president happened to us, as well?"

Contillo made a grand gesture. "All of you will have the honor of dying in the line of duty. And if I do say so myself, you should be grateful. The president will probably give you a medal. Posthumously, of course."

"El Gato?" Lazalde asked.

The colonel and the drug lord traded smug expressions. "Why, there was no trace of him at all, my dear. I will tell the president that we looked and looked and never found any hidden sub base."

Lazalde shook with suppressed rage. "You are devious scum, I will grant you that. But one day someone will hold you to account for your crimes."

Contillo laughed.

Quesada kicked Ramirez, knocking the young officer onto his side. "Enough idle talk," he said. "I want this worthless pile of flesh fed to the caimans." He gripped Lazalde by the chin and made a show of examining her. "As for you, woman, you are quite pretty for a soldier. I will have some fun with you before you join your friend."

Bolan saw the lieutenant draw back her leg to kick Quesada, but she wasn't fast enough. He shoved her down so hard that she cracked her head and lay dazed. The Executioner put a hand on the Beretta. Quesada, though, didn't inflict further harm. Instead, he faced his underling, Tejo.

"Take the woman to my quarters. Have Stenson dump the soldier in the river. Then have four men search the cavern from top to bottom for the American."

"But he was blown to pieces, boss," the triggerman protested. "I saw it with my own eyes."

"But *I* did not," Quesada said. "And I have not survived as long as I have by taking things for granted. You will conduct a thorough search, and then you will get back to me. Fast."

"Yes, sir," Tejo said meekly. At a sharp jerk of the hardman's wrist, two gunners seized Ramirez and dragged the limp figure toward the pens.

There was nothing Bolan could do for the man. His main priority now was to detonate the charges and get out of there alive, with the lieutenant. Thinking a moment, he set the timers on both devices for ten minutes. It wasn't much time, but it would have to do. Any longer, and he risked the search party finding them.

Taking another packet of plastique and a third detonator with him, Bolan padded toward the small building where Lazalde was being taken. A pair of hardmen thrust her inside and emerged thirty seconds later, closing the door behind them.

Over by the big structure, Quesada and Contillo were in the middle of a heated debate. Why, Bolan didn't know, but he could use it to his advantage. Hurrying around to the side of the small building, he peered in a window. Through cracked blinds he saw Lazalde slumped in a chair, a rope around her shoulders, another securing her legs.

There was no back way in. Bolan eased to the front corner. Quesada and the colonel were gone, and no gunners were close by. Tucking his chin to his chest to hide his face, he strolled to the door and quickly ducked inside.

Lazalde looked up, the fear in her eyes changing to relief. "Señor Belasko!" she breathed. "They claimed that you were dead!"

"There's a saying in my country," Bolan whispered, crouching in front of her and snaking the Ka-bar knife from its sheath. "Don't count your chickens until they're hatched." He cut the rope holding her to the chair, then the rope binding her wrists.

"We have a similar saying," she said, rising unsteadily.

The door opened.

Bolan was on one knee, the knife still in his right hand, the detonator and explosive by his left foot. He whirled, rising, thinking one of the underlings had caught them but it was the head man himself, Estavan Quesada.

His reputation was justly deserved. The instant he saw the Executioner, his right hand streaked under his jacket and flashed out, holding the blade he had used on Ramirez. He took a bound and slashed, so lightning quick that the human eye could barely follow his movements.

Bolan parried the swing. Their blades rang together, and he danced backward to have room to maneuver.

Lazalde gripped the chair and went to raise it. Quesada, never breaking stride, executed a sterling spin kick. The lieutenant was flung off her feet and crashed to the floor beside a desk. She made a feeble attempt to rise, then collapsed.

Aware that there wasn't a second to waste, Bolan speared his knife at his foe's chest. The Colombian evaded it with ease, shifted and nearly cut Bolan from ear to ear. The soldier circled, holding the Ka-bar knife low, trying to tempt Quesada into striking.

But the man wasn't about to take the bait. Shifting the blade from hand to hand, his white, even teeth bared in a mocking smirk, he matched the Executioner's every step, keeping an arm's length between them, waiting for an opening to exploit.

At least a minute and a half had gone by since Bolan set the charges. He calculated it would take him two minutes to reach the water safely, another three to swim to the entrance before the explosives went off. He had to eliminate Quesada and get Lazalde out of there.

Quesada suddenly threw back his head and roared, "Tejo! Guillermo! It's the American! Get in here!"

Bolan tensed. No one answered. The door had swung shut after Quesada entered, so it was possible no one had heard. To prevent the drug lord from yelling again, Bolan skipped in close and slashed at Quesada's torso. The man twisted, feinted and struck at the soldier's neck.

Ducking, Bolan spun out of reach, then side-stepped. Now he was near the door and Quesada was a few steps from Lazalde. The drug czar regarded him coldly.

"You are good, American. Better than most."

The tall man's English was impeccable. Bolan's response was to whip his left hand to the speed rig under his left arm.

Quesada flicked the blade, nearly opening Bolan's hand from knuckles to wrist, forcing the Executioner to yank down his arm before he could draw the Beretta.

"Try that again, American, and you lose fingers. I guarantee."

Bolan didn't doubt it, nor could he try for the Desert Eagle on his right hip. To draw it, he would have to let go of the Ka-bar knife. That left the P-11, which had slid around behind him. Could he reach it before his adversary struck?

Lazalde moaned.

Quesada didn't glance at her. He was too skilled to take his eyes off Bolan for even an instant. But the solider could see that the drug lord was concerned she would revive, making it two against one. He sidled to the right in order to keep them both in sight.

Bolan was running out of time. Their stalemate would result in Lazalde's death and his own unless he did something, and did it right away. Quesada gave him a clue what to do.

"You will never get out of here alive, American. Surrender, and I will make your end swift."

"We'll die together," Bolan responded. "I've planted plastique charges set to go off in just a few minutes." The soldier's intention was to shock Quesada into lowering his guard. It was a gambit that failed.

The man twirled with all the speed of his namesake, took two long bounds, threw his arms over his head and hurtled at the window as if blasted from a howitzer. He smashed through the blinds and the glass, and dropped.

Bolan didn't lose another second. Racing to the lieutenant, he boosted her to her feet. Lazalde's eyes fluttered open, but she was too groggy to walk under her own power so he propelled her to the door.

Quiet reigned outside, but not for long. Quesada's voice rose from the rear of the building. Shouting broke out, attended by the pounding of feet.

Clasping Lazalde about the waist, Bolan gained the temporary shelter of a stack of crates before anyone appeared. He shook her to bring her around, whispering, "Snap out of it! We have to get out of here! I've already set the charges!"

The lieutenant's eyes cleared. She heard the yells and the commotion and said, "Lead the way. I will be right behind you."

Taking her at her word, Bolan pivoted and sped toward the sub pens. Setting additional charges was out of the question. He had to hope that the ones already in place were enough to do the job.

A siren went off, and in the background the chopper's rotors hummed to life, spinning faster and faster. From one end of the cavern to the other, men cried out in rising panic.

Bolan wasn't about to try to swim from the cavern. They'd never make it. Reaching the forklift, he sheathed his knife and drew the 9 mm pistol and the Desert Eagle. Then, nodding at Lazalde, he burst into the open, streaking toward the patrol boat.

Smugglers were scurrying every which way. Several raced past Bolan without giving him a second glance. He slowed as he neared the dock and saw someone about to step onto the patrol boat.

It was Sergeant Mendoza. The noncom spotted Bolan, grabbed for his SMG, slung over his right shoulder and started to level it.

Bolan stroked the Beretta's trigger twice. At each cough of the suppressor, Mendoza's fatigue shirt sprouted holes. The renegade noncom staggered, spun and toppled into the water beside the hull.

Two gunners materialized from out of nowhere. Bolan nailed one with the 9 mm pistol, the other with the Desert Eagle. The boom of the .44 Magnum gun was nearly eclipsed by the strident scream of the siren. Halting at the bow of the boat, he motioned for Lazalde to hop in. "Start it up!" he ordered. "I'll cover you."

To the east men were scrambling into a minisub. To the west another submersible was getting under way. It slipped its berth and headed for the entrance, only to lurch to a stop at the end of a mooring line. In their haste to flee, the crew had neglected to cast off.

The canvas that covered the opening, which had

been lowered after Mendoza arrived, was slowly rising.

Bolan backed toward the patrol boat as the engine snarled, then caught. Suddenly slugs stitched the dock at his feet, fired by a gangly triggerman perched on a crate. Resting the barrel of the Desert Eagle on top of the Beretta to steady his aim, Bolan fired once.

The gunner reacted as if kicked by a mule. Jacknifing into the water, he sank without a murmur.

"Jump on!" Lazalde shouted.

Bolan ran to the bowline. Quickly he unwound it from its cleat and cast it onto the boat. As he rose, the lieutenant yelled, "Behind you!"

Three smugglers were barreling toward him. Bolan pegged one with a snap shot from the Beretta. Rolling onto his shoulder as bullets gouged into the dock, he trained the Desert Eagle on a second triggerman and perforated the man's brain from forehead to spine. The third smuggler frantically backpedaled, but the big .44 took off the top of the gunner's skull in a scarlet spray of blood, bone and hair.

By this time two minisubs were heading for open water while others were in the process of vacating their pens. The motorboat roared past them, Stenson hunched beside the outboard.

As Bolan sprang onto the patrol boat, Colonel Contillo's chopper lifted into the air, banked and sped toward the cavern's gaping maw. Lazalde threw the boat into reverse, and once they cleared their berth, she opened the throttle.

The Executioner stared at the fuel pump. He had lost all track of time but knew it couldn't be much longer before the fireworks went off. The boat covered twenty yards, then forty.

Three more subs were churning toward the river.

"I think we are going to make it!" Lazalde declared.

All hell broke loose.

A tremendous explosion rocked the cavern as the fuel pump went up. A blistering fireball seared toward the roof, expanding in a span of heartbeats into a blazing mushroom cloud. The concussion from the blast tore corrugated metal to ribbons and crushed everything in its path.

The blast was at its apex when another explosion erupted. Either the torpedoes or the ammunition or both coalesced into a secondary explosion more violent than the first. The entire cavern floor shook, jumped and cracked wide open in a score of places. Flames shot thirty feet high.

Dozens of smugglers, desperately striving to pile onto minisubs and a few motorboats, were reduced to charred flesh where they stood. Others, their clothes ablaze, dived screaming into the water.

The patrol boat lurched, nearly spilling Bolan over the side. He saw the water roil, clouds of black smoke billowing toward them and huge stalactites rain down from above. A sub was hit by three of them, one right after the other, warping deck plates at the waterline. Water poured into the gap. In moments smoke rose from the stricken vessel.

"Hold on!" Lazalde shouted. She spun the wheel to avoid a stalactite, turning it again to stay on an even keel.

More explosions spelled the beginning of the end. Whole sections of the roof started to split off and fall. An enormous chunk landed on a motorboat, pulverizing it and its occupants.

A block of stone smashed into the water next to them. Waves six feet high washed over the gunwale, catching the officer off guard and flinging her against the console. Bolan leaped, gripping the wheel before they swerved out of control. He brought them back onto an even plane, revved the engine to stabilize the sputtering carburetor and roared toward the entrance.

The debris from the crumbling roof had become a torrent. A minisub was hit astern by a slab that rivaled a refrigerator in shape and size. Metal crumpled like paper. The vessel sloughed, then slowed to a crawl. Crewmen popped out of the top hatch. They were clustered on the narrow afterdeck, speaking excitedly, when the sub unexpectedly rolled over. Just like that, they were gone.

Bolan zigzagged to avoid the lethal downpour. So much smoke and dust filled the air that he could no longer see the opening. He had to rely on his instincts and hope they were on course.

Seconds later the cavern quaked to a deafening noise overhead. There was thunderous crackling and snapping and crunching, then a sound reminiscent of an avalanche. Glancing back, Bolan glimpsed fully a third of the roof caving in. "Grab on to something!" he yelled.

A tidal wave overtook them, lifted them, carried them on its crest. No matter which way Bolan spun the wheel, the patrol boat surged straight ahead. To

the east a minisub foundered and went under. A
smaller boat capsized and was shredded. White spray
drenched Bolan as they passed under the canvas.

The patrol boat was swept hundreds of feet from
the former cavern on a sheet of water. Gradually the
wave lost its momentum. The boat slowed and set-
tled. Bolan let up on the throttle and also let out the
breath, which he hadn't realized he was holding.

"We did it!" Lazalde whooped, throwing herself
into his arms. "We are safe at last!"

The Executioner looked around.

No, they weren't.

15

Bolan and Lazalde weren't the only ones who had lived through the ordeal.

Circling low over the water, its spotlight sweeping over the surface, was Colonel Contillo's chopper. The bright beam illuminated Stenson's motorboat, then roved on to reveal two minisubs that had emerged unscathed. On the foredeck of one stood Estavan Quesada and Tejo, surveying the Patia River.

So far no one had noticed the patrol boat. "We're not out of the woods yet," Bolan said, then bent to the wheel.

The brilliant spotlight stabbed at them, impaling the patrol boat in its harsh glare. Frowning, Bolan cut to the left but the spotlight stayed with their craft.

Stenson turned the motorboat in their direction and lifted the AK-47.

El Gato and Tejo disappeared down the hatch of their sub. Within moments the vessel looped toward the patrol boat. The other minisub promptly did the same.

Lazalde swore. "They are all coming after us! We will never get away!"

"Take the wheel and head down the river," Bolan

ordered. Automatically she obeyed, and he stepped to the Browning. Yanking back the bolt, he gripped the handles and swung the heavy machine gun around until the front blade sight fixed squarely on the oncoming motorboat.

Compared to most machine guns, the M-2 had a slow cyclic rate of less than five hundred rounds per minute. That meant it couldn't penetrate heavy armor. But the .50-caliber workhorse was a holy terror against anything short of a tank, as Bolan demonstrated by opening up on the motorboat at a range of only 150 feet.

Stenson had just triggered the AK-47. He was bucked backward by the firestorm of heavy slugs that punched holes as big as fifty-cent pieces in his body and the motorboat. His leg caught on the outboard. Dead on his feet, he toppled over the stern as the boat, swiftly taking on water, veered out of control.

Bolan swiveled the Browning on its tripod and elevated the barrel toward the helicopter. The pilot hadn't yet realized his mistake and was holding the spotlight steady on the patrol boat. Bolan squeezed, and the big .50-caliber gun boomed. There were no tracer rounds to tell if he was on target, but judging by the way the chopper suddenly shuddered and dipped, he had scored a hit.

The soldier sighted down the barrel again. Tilting wildly, the helicopter swooped to the northwest, climbing to gain altitude. It was out of range in moments.

Two down, two to go, Bolan mused as he swung the M-2 around. With the spotlight no longer lighting up the scene, the two minisubs were vague shapes in the darkness, bearing down on the patrol boat at fifteen to twenty knots.

The Executioner fired, and he could hear the scream of ricochets above the growl of the patrol boat's engine. He had no way of knowing if any of the rounds penetrated, but since the minisub never slowed, he had to conclude that the M-2 was having little effect. Either that or Quesada thirsted for revenge, no matter what.

The patrol boat raced into the narrow neck of the river and fishtailed as Lazalde took the first hairpin turn much too fast. She compensated and they flew onward. The hull bumped something in the water that jarred the entire boat. Seconds later it happened again. Lazalde glanced at her companion. "What—"

"Caimans," Bolan replied.

She began to pull back on the throttle.

"Do that, and Quesada will cram a torpedo right up our stern," he warned.

"You had better take the wheel, then," Lazalde said. "I do not have much experience with boats."

Bolan moved toward her but stopped as Contillo's helicopter flashed in at treetop level from the north. The spotlight pegged them, and an SMG chattered. Thankfully the gunner was a bit too hasty. The slugs overshot, peppering the surface beside them.

The soldier tried to bring the M-2 to bear, but the chopper was gone before he could fire. It would be back, though—of that he was certain—so he stayed put, scanning the sky, while Lazalde sped down the river.

It would have been easy for them to avoid the caimans if they switched on their running lights, but that would also make it easier for their enemies to spot them.

Bolan tried not to think of what would happen should they hit a submerged log or one of the twenty-foot anacondas so numerous along the Patia. It might well wreck the boat and leave them at the mercy of the river's savage denizens, or El Gato.

The minisubs were still back there. Every so often Bolan glimpsed the inky outlines of their conning towers and a hint of fine spray off their decks. As yet, the vessels hadn't fired a single torpedo. With all the twists and bends in the waterway, they would only be wasted. But downriver were several long straight stretches. If Quesada could keep the patrol boat in sight, that was when he would attack.

On open water the patrol boat could handily have outdistanced the submersibles. As it was, they were gaining ground all too slowly.

Several minutes went by, and the helicopter failed to reappear. Bolan took a gamble and shouldered the lieutenant aside. "Allow me," he said, increasing speed.

"Be my guest."

Lazalde tried the radio but picked up only static. Again and again she tried to raise the destroyer, with no luck. "We must have taken a hit," she speculated.

Bolan had another theory. The unit might have been sabotaged before they even left the ship to prevent them from contacting the outside world. He distinctly recalled that the colonel had ordered Ramirez not to raise the destroyer unless it was an emergency, so not once on the way up the Patia had the captain broken radio silence.

A bend loomed before them, and Bolan had to throttle back. He swung wide around the point of land and kept alert for objects in their path. Without lights, he couldn't see more than a dozen feet, so he had to be ready at an instant's notice to kill the engine.

The sound of rotor blades heralded the return of the chopper. This time the pilot flew in over the river directly in front of them, and hovered. Someone holding an SMG leaned out the side.

"Get down!" Bolan hollered as the windshield spiderwebbed and lead zinged past his shoulders. He swerved to the right, then to the left. The helicopter dipped and bobbed so the gunner wouldn't lose sight of the boat. Rounds thudded into the bow and sent slivers of wood flying.

Bolan could guess what Contillo was up to. The colonel wanted to pin them down long enough for the minisubs to catch up and finish them off.

Lazalde brought the Browning into play, but her accuracy left a lot to be desired. The swaying boat compounded her difficulty.

Abruptly bringing the patrol craft broadside to the helicopter, Bolan leaped to the machine gun. Lazalde relinquished her hold without being asked, and he slipped in behind the tripod. The gunner on the chopper unleashed a short burst that chipped wood off the gunwale. Bolan returned fire and had the satisfaction of seeing the man grip his chest and plummet from the aircraft.

The pilot could take a hint. Rotors shrieking, the chopper arced upward, then headed due north.

Bolan rushed to the control console. The submarines would be on them soon unless they got out of there. He brought the bow around and accelerated. A bulky reptilian form in the river caused him to veer close to the right bank to avoid it.

He racked his brain for a way out of the situation. Being outnumbered was bad enough; being outgunned was a graver handicap. In the case of the helicopter, the patrol boat lacked the speed to outrun it. In the case of the minisubs, the boat's firepower was hardly adequate to put a dent in their hulls.

The depth charges would do the job, except for two hitches. They were designed for subsurface use and were rigged to go off at a certain depth. Worse, their launchers were designed to hurl the charges to either side of the patrol craft, not to the rear, which happened to be the direction the enemy was coming from.

Bolan had always been a master tactician, but in this instance he was stumped. How could he turn the patrol boat's shortcomings to their benefit?

The soldier negotiated a series of turns. He saw the helicopter shadowing them a prudent distance to the north. A surface-to-air missile would have come in handy right about then.

Bolan tried to remember where the Patia's tributaries had been. They were virtually impossible to spot in the pitch black of night. To increase his chances, he moved closer to the south shore. "Keep your eyes peeled for a stream, Maria," he said.

"I will," she answered.

Another kink in the river necessitated slowing down. Beyond was a straightaway. Bolan snapped the throttle to the maximum, and the bow rose into the air. For hundreds of yards they cleaved the water smoothly, the helicopter making no attempt to stop them. Peculiar, Bolan thought, until his companion yelled.

"Behind us!" Lazalde said. "Isn't that one of the subs?"

Bolan looked and saw that the minisub had reached the straight belt of river and had a clear shot. He searched for sign of the next bend, but it was still a ways off.

"A torpedo is closing in!" the lieutenant cried.

The Executioner shifted. Sixty feet back something long, slender and moving fast glinted just under the surface.

A crook in the river promised salvation if they could reach it before the torpedo reached them.

"It's gaining!" Lazalde warned.

Bolan knew it would. He was going much too fast to take the next turn safely, but he didn't care. It was either that or be blown to kingdom come. "Hang on!" he cautioned, and rocketed into the tight bend doing more than forty knots.

Wildly rotating the wheel with both hands, Bolan struggled to keep the boat under control. It was hopeless. The craft shot broadside toward the south bank. The hull thudded into a knob of low ground rife with reeds, bounced off intact and tore down the river at the same second that the torpedo plowed into the bend.

The darkness was briefly relieved by the burst of vivid light that marked the explosion. Mud, pieces of vegetation and water cascaded down, narrowly missing the patrol boat.

In the glow of the blast, Bolan spied an opening on his left. Not knowing if it was a tributary or simply a place where the bank had buckled, he drastically reduced speed and steered into it. Foliage immediately closed over them. They had stumbled on a stream.

Bolan shut off the engine and turned. A swishing sound and the muted churning of a prop came from the river. A metallic hulk sailed past, followed in no time at all by another.

"They will never find us now!" Lazalde commented.

Once again she had spoken too soon. Rotors whirred overhead as the chopper flashed in over the trees seeking them. The spotlight pierced the gloom but missed the patrol boat and roved southward.

Bolan scrambled to pivot the Browning and elevate the muzzle to the right angle. A lot of limbs and vines were in the way, but that didn't stop him from letting the heavy machine gun voice its deadly cacophony once more.

The tail pylon was ratcheted from the fuselage to the horizontal stabilizer. Sparks flew. As if thrown by heavy turbulence, the helicopter listed to one side. That gave Bolan a shot at the engine cowling and he took it, raking the cowl from the turbine to the rotary fairing. He kept firing as the chopper tilted at a steep angle. It recovered and tried to gain altitude, smoke pouring from the engine. The rotors chugged instead of whined; the cockpit angled downward.

Bolan didn't linger to see what would happen next. Odds were that Contillo was in radio contact with Quesada. So now the drug lord knew that the patrol boat was behind the submarines, not in front of them, and he would be taking steps accordingly. Bolan revved the engine, barreled out from under cover and headed down the Patia at full speed.

The helicopter had leveled off only a few yards above the trees. Its tail swung crazily from side to side, and its rotors were spinning slower by the second. The pilot made one last effort to get the nose up, but all he succeeded in doing was sending the chopper into free fall. It smashed into the jungle and went up like a Roman candle, showering fiery shards of metal in all directions.

"Good riddance!" Lazalde breathed.

Bolan shared her sentiments but was too busy to comment. Ahead were many twists and turns he had to watch out for. He leaned close to the shattered windshield in the hope of glimpsing the submarines, but they were nowhere to be seen.

Trying to put himself in Quesada's shoes, Bolan debated whether the man would turn and fight or make a run for the Pacific Ocean. Quesada wanted revenge for the destruction of his sub base, but with Contillo gone, and a destroyer at anchor near the mouth of the Patia River, Quesada would do the smart thing and head for the open sea. Once safe, he would no doubt rebuild his operation with ill-gotten gains from the drug trade. In a year or so his organization would be up and running at full steam.

Not if Bolan could help it. The Executioner held the patrol boat to a reckless rate, negotiating every bend three times as fast as they had on their journey inland.

Lazalde joined him at the wheel. "Why do you not turn on our running lights? The helicopter is gone. It would be safe to do so."

"I don't want Quesada to know where we are until we're right on top of him," Bolan replied.

"He will know anyway. His radar will tell him."

Bolan didn't blame her for being anxious. They invited disaster by not slowing down. But if they did, they would lose their quarry for sure. "There are so many twists in this river that his radar is only good for short distances. We should be able to take him by surprise."

"I sincerely hope so, Señor Belasko. After going through all we did back there, I would hate to die by crashing into an alligator or a tree. It would be a stupid way to go, no?"

She had a point, but Bolan was committed. He buckled down to the task of catching the minisubs. Ten minutes passed with no sign of them. Twenty minutes, and still no conning towers knifed the water in the distance. Half an hour, and Bolan harbored grave concern. Something was very wrong. He should have overtaken Quesada by then.

The Executioner remembered passing another tributary. Had Quesada used his own ruse against him and ducked into it until the patrol boat went by? Acting on a hunch, Bolan angled to the right and brought the craft to a standstill next to an earthen bank. He put the gear in neutral so the engine idled quietly. "Do we have any grenades on board?" he asked Lazalde.

"I think Captain Ramirez brought some in his backpack. Do you want them?"

"Right away."

It was just as Bolan had deduced. As Lazalde stepped to where the gear was stowed, the first mini-sub materialized as a stovepipe silhouette moving rapidly down the center of the river. On its heels came the second.

No one was on deck on either.

The patrol boat was so close to shore that Bolan counted on their radar not picking it up until it was too late. He opened up the craft as the second mini-sub came abreast of their position, gluing his bow to its prop wash. "Hurry with those grenades," he directed.

The crew of the second sub didn't take long to discover they had a shadow. The top hatch clanged open and a man holding an Uzi popped out.

Bolan had anticipated them. He had the Desert Eagle braced on the rim of the windshield. Thumbing back the hammer, he fired repeatedly, emptying the clip. The gunner didn't appear to be hit but he did duck down the hatch, which was just what Bolan wanted.

"Here you are."

The lieutenant held three grenades, resembling the L-2 A-1 that was common with British forces.

"Fuse delay?" Bolan needed to know.

"Four seconds."

It wasn't much, but they had to do. Bolan took one and gestured for her to assume control of the patrol boat. "When I give the word, bring us up next to the sub."

"What do you have in mind?"

Bolan drew the Beretta and moved to the port gunwale. Placing a foot on it, he coiled his legs. "Hurry, before they submerge on us!"

"You can't mean to—"

The rest of her words were lost in a rush of air and dank spray as Bolan vaulted onto the minisub's afterdeck. He slipped, nearly sprawling into the river. Righting himself, he sprang to the ladder. As he cleared the top, the gunner reappeared, the man's shock at finding Bolan on the sub paralyzing him for the heartbeat of time it took Bolan to squeeze the Beretta's trigger.

The drug runner fell from view.

Bolan squatted at the hatch, hearing arguing voices coming from below. He pulled the pin on the grenade, verified that Lazalde had the patrol boat alongside the vessel and let go. A short step brought him to the edge. He vaulted into space, shouting in midair, "Go! Go!"

The Executioner's boots smacked onto the deck as the patrol boat leaped forward, pitching him onto his elbows and knees. In his mind he ticked off the seconds.

The minisub's hull muffled the explosion. It was more like the pop of a firecracker than a grenade going off. Smoke and fire spewed from the hatch. The vessel canted to the left and at twelve knots rammed into the bank, buckling the bow and flipping the submersible onto its side.

"After the other one!" Bolan commanded, grabbing another grenade from the seat where the lieutenant had placed them.

Lazalde tried her best, but Quesada was submerging his vessel. The deck and the lower half of the conning tower slipped smoothly under as Bolan cocked an arm. The Executioner checked his swing rather than risk missing and waste the grenade.

Yet another bend slowed both boats. Bolan recognized a spindly tree at the water's edge and knew that the next stage of the river was broad and deep. The sub would be able to go all the way under, and they would lose it.

The lieutenant glanced at him. "Now is our chance!" she had to shout to be heard. "Use the depth charges!"

Doubting it would do any good, Bolan responded. "At what depth are they rigged to go off?"

Lazalde smiled grimly. "They're contact chargés!"

Bolan swung around. Contact charges detonated when they bumped up against anything hard. So even if he missed the minisub, the depth charge would go off when it hit the bottom and just might catch the submersible in the radius of its blast. He ran to the port launcher and leaned down to better study the controls.

It was set to fire, and the press of a button was all it would take.

Just the antenna array on the sub was visible, and even that soon vanished in a bubbling sheet of foam. The lieutenant pushed the patrol boat to its limit, streaking to the right of the minisub's wake. Suddenly she pointed straight ahead. "What's that?"

Only then did Bolan see another boat seventy feet in front of them. It took a moment for the configuration to register as another submarine. It was the one that had passed them as they wound up the Patia.

As Bolan set eyes on the minisub, it began to dive. He wondered if Quesada was aware of it, and if the skipper of the second sub was aware of the approaching vessel. As things stood, the two minisubs were on a collision course.

Inspiration galvanized the Executioner into action. If something was to momentarily confuse the sonar on the two minisubs, they just might smash into each other.

"Don't stop!" Bolan shouted, touching his finger to the launcher. The patrol boat streaked past where he believed Quesada's sub to be. At the instant they came abreast of the open space between the two minisubs, he fired the depth charge.

The patrol craft sped westward, but Bolan never took his gaze off the depth charge. He saw it splash down and sink. In the time he could have counted to three, the river erupted skyward as if spewed forth by an underwater volcano. A second disturbance boiled the water moments later, followed by a third that gushed untold gallons upward, like a geyser.

"Slow down and turn around," Bolan directed. Claiming his M-16, he switched on the running lights and roved a small spotlight mounted on the foredeck over the surface.

An oil slick was spreading rapidly. Part of the second minisub protruded above the surface, its hull shattered, an electric arc dancing around the gaping hole.

There was no sign of Estavan Quesada's boat, but Bolan knew that the Cat had finally run out of lives. He knew because three bodies bobbed up, and one, although headless, wore the remains of a well-cut suit and had gold rings on every finger.

"Did we do it?" Lazalde asked breathlessly.

"We did it," Bolan confirmed. "Let's go home."

**The Stony Man commandos deliver hard justice
to a dispenser of death**

STONY MAN™ 33

PUNITIVE MEASURES

The Eliminator—a cheaply made yet effective handgun
that's being mass-produced and distributed underground—
is turning up in the hands of street gangs and criminals
throughout the world. As the grisly death toll rises, the
Stony Man teams mount an international dragnet against a
mastermind who knows that death is cheap. Now he's
about to discover that Stony Man gives retribution
away—free.

Available in February 1998 at your favorite retail outlet.

A deadly kind of immortality...

THE

Destroyer™

#110 Never Say Die

Created by
WARREN MURPHY
and RICHARD SAPIR

Forensic evidence in a number of assassinations reveals a curious link between the killers: identical fingerprints and genetic code. The bizarre problem is turned over to Remo and Chiun, who follow the trail back to a literal dead end— the grave of an executed killer.

Look for it in January wherever Gold Eagle books are sold.

**A violent struggle for survival
in a post-holocaust world**

JAMES AXLER

DEATH LANDS®

Freedom Lost

Following up rumors of trouble on his old home ground, Ryan and
his band seek shelter inside the walls of what was once the largest
shopping mall in the Carolinas. The baron of the fortress gives them
no choice but to join his security detail. As outside invaders step up
their raids on the mall, Ryan must battle both sides for a chance to
save their lives.

James Axler

OUTLANDERS™

OMEGA PATH

A dark and unfathomable power governs
post-nuclear America. As a former warrior of
the secretive regime, Kane races to expose the
blueprint of a power that's immeasurably evil,
with the aid of fellow outcasts Brigid Baptiste
and Grant. In a pre-apocalyptic New York City,
hope lies in their ability to reach one young
man who can perhaps alter the future....

Nothing is as it seems. Not even the
invincible past....

Available February 1998,
wherever Gold Eagle books are sold.

Don't miss out on the action in these titles featuring THE EXECUTIONER®, STONY MAN™ and SUPERBOLAN®!

The American Trilogy

#64222	PATRIOT GAMBIT	$3.75 U.S.	☐
		$4.25 CAN.	☐
#64223	HOUR OF CONFLICT	$3.75 U.S.	☐
		$4.25 CAN.	☐
#64224	CALL TO ARMS	$3.75 U.S.	☐
		$4.25 CAN.	☐

Stony Man™

#61910	FLASHBACK	$5.50 U.S.	☐
		$6.50 CAN.	☐
#61911	ASIAN STORM	$5.50 U.S.	☐
		$6.50 CAN.	☐
#61912	BLOOD STAR	$5.50 U.S.	☐
		$6.50 CAN.	☐

SuperBolan®

#61452	DAY OF THE VULTURE	$5.50 U.S.	☐
		$6.50 CAN.	☐
#61453	FLAMES OF WRATH	$5.50 U.S.	☐
		$6.50 CAN.	☐
#61454	HIGH AGGRESSION	$5.50 U.S.	☐
		$6.50 CAN.	☐

(limited quantities available on certain titles)

TOTAL AMOUNT	$
POSTAGE & HANDLING	$
($1.00 for one book, 50¢ for each additional)	
APPLICABLE TAXES*	$ _____
TOTAL PAYABLE	$ _____
(check or money order—please do not send cash)	

To order, complete this form and send it, along with a check or money order for the total above, payable to Gold Eagle Books, to: **In the U.S.:** 3010 Walden Avenue, P.O. Box 9077, Buffalo, NY 14269-9077; **In Canada:** P.O. Box 636, Fort Erie, Ontario, L2A 5X3.

Name: _____

Address: _____ City: _____

State/Prov.: _____ Zip/Postal Code: _____

*New York residents remit applicable sales taxes.
 Canadian residents remit applicable GST and provincial taxes.

GOLD EAGLE®

GEBACK19